Ruby's Last Chance

by

Joy Wood

Dedication

To my husband, John . . . the wind beneath my wings.

1.

"Morning Ruby," her colleague Sophie, a photographer at the newspaper greeted her in the kitchenette off the main office. "Coffee?" she asked filling the kettle from the tap.

"Yeah, please." Ruby leant against the worktop, "It's been a bloody nightmare this morning. The gropers are out in force on the Tube – one arse grab and one thrust up against me. Honestly, one of these days I swear I'm going to take a fake gun with me and the next bloke that thinks it's okay to touch me up, shove it in his crotch, just for the shock factor."

"I like your style," Sophie grinned, "but you'll probably end up with some sort of charge for threatening with a fake weapon. A good old knee to the nuts might be safer . . . and more gratifying."

Ruby laughed. "You're right. Do you know what, I'd love to follow them home, knock on their doors and tell their wives what they're up to. Can you imagine that? I'm sick to death of them thinking it's acceptable to touch women up."

"You and me both and half the population of females riding the underground during rush hour. I remember once a woman shouting in her loudest voice, *get your filthy hands off my backside, now.* The bloke's face was a picture –

he scurried off at the next stop. I wish I had the courage to be so bold."

Ruby couldn't help but snigger, "Maybe I should try that next time."

"Yeah, or like I said a good old fashioned knee to the nuts." Sophie spooned instant coffee into the cups and filled them with boiling water, "How did Friday go by the way? Did you manage to sort things out when you were off?"

"Not sure about sort out," Ruby widened her eyes as she took the milk out of the fridge and handed it to Sophie, "but I've got myself a bit of breathing space with a payment plan for the two credit card companies, and my dad has transferred me some money to tide me over for my rent, bless him. So for now, I'm okay, at least for the next couple of months – I just won't be able to afford to eat or drink anything. Thanks," she took her mug from Sophie, a delightful Christmas present she'd got in the secret Santa with an embossed logo of *Reading between the wines*.

"God, Richie's really left you in the cart, hasn't he? I'm guessing you still have no idea where the moron is?"

"No, he's long gone, along with anything of value. I'd need more than a fake gun if I ever set eyes on him again. His other girlfriend has texted a couple of times, she's desperately trying to find him. I've told her if she does, to let me know."

"Do you reckon she will?"

"Nah, I doubt it. He's left her like me, with debts. I don't think somehow there'll be any sort of trail. His type are clever and no doubt have done this sort of thing before."

"What a bastard, eh, two girlfriends at the same time. He was certainly an accomplished liar."

"Oh, yeah, he was that. He's put a brand new meaning to the term working away from home. Anyway, let's not talk about him, he's not worth it." She took a sip of her coffee, "How's things with you? Has your mother arrived?"

"Yeah, she's finally here, that's why I'm in so early. She's taken charge of Lilly and managed in two days to make me feel like I'm the worst mother in the world. Seemingly, I'm not doing things right at all. I should have a regular bedtime routine now and feeds at set times. Her favourite word is routine. I'm telling you, if I hear it one more time, never mind getting her a train ticket home, I'll be driving her myself. Lee's had enough already, reckons he might have to book himself in a Premier Inn or something. He can't stand her for longer than a day or so."

"Aww, that's a shame," Ruby said, "I bet she's not that bad."

"She's alright, she means well. You know Lee though, he's a bit," Sophie scowled attempting to find the right expression, "socially awkward."

Never was a truer word spoken, although Ruby thought socially awkward was a bit polite. Odd described Lee much better. She couldn't understand how her level-headed friend had hooked up with him in the first place. He wasn't dynamic boyfriend material by any means. But he'd met Sophie when she was already pregnant with Lilly and deserved some credit for taking on another man's child. And at the end of the day, what sort of judge was she about men after the disaster she'd had with Richie who'd left her completely high and dry?

"I hardly dare ask," Ruby pulled a pained face, "anything from your last solicitor's letter?"

"Only a one-liner from a swanky New York solicitor with a classy logo, saying De'Ath refutes parenthood of Lilly and stiffly finishing with a warning not to contact him again or he'd be taking legal action against me."

"Shit. So what happens now?"

"I honestly don't know. Lee's adamant we don't give up. And he's right. Lilly's life will be much better if I can get some maintenance money. That's all I want, I'm not asking him to be involved if he doesn't want to. He'll have to answer to his daughter when she's old enough. But it's going to be costly taking the great Edward De'Ath on. And even though Lee is dead set on pursuing him, we don't have the sort of money that'll take. It could run into thousands."

"It's not right," Ruby sipped her coffee, "he is Lilly's father, he needs to support his daughter and have a relationship with her."

"That's never gonna happen if he's denying everything. And I guess it's easy to understand from his point of view, a drunken one-night stand in a London hotel and parenthood nine months later. Who would willingly own up to it and spend the next eighteen years paying maintenance when it's much easier to deny? My mother will have something to say about it once she gets settled, I know she will. She's said before she'll help us financially, but she hasn't got a massive load of savings so I don't want to take what little she's got. At the end of the day, I can't prove he is the father; it's my word against his. He's hardly likely to come forward of his own accord to do any tests and I can't afford to make him through the courts."

"It's just not fair, is it? Just shows there's one rule for the rich, and one for the rest of us."

"Yeah, you're right there. Hey, I've just remembered," Sophie pulled the door to the small kitchenette closed and lowered her voice, "I think Neil has something going on. He's been huddled in his office with Millicent magnificent since I got here. When I was taking my coat off, he came through to the main office and said to tell you as soon as you arrive, to go and see him. So, I reckon he has another one of those classic jobs with your name on it."

"Oh, God no," Ruby blew out a breath, "I can't face another. I'd rather report on Fred's allotment and his magical mix horse manure for his roses, or Jack's gaping hole in the roof of his pigeon loft . . . anything so I don't have to get a story from another middle-aged man who thinks he's the spitting image of Brad Pitt when in reality he's more like Chewbacca. I tell you, I'm not doing any more. And I'm going to tell Neil that."

"I can't say I blame you. You shouldn't have to, but I guess you've little choice with all the debt Richie's left you with. Maybe for now you've just got to grin and bear it and keep taking the money. Until you get yourself straight, that is."

Ruby scratched her creased forehead, "Yeah, but that's easier said than done after Saturday night."

"Why, what happened Saturday night?"

"Let's just say it didn't end well."

"Oh, hell. I thought Neil looked a bit like he was chewing a wasp this morning. Go on, tell me."

The kitchen door swung open, "There you are, Ruby," Millicent Mawer, the paper's senior reporter said, addressing her like she was a naughty schoolgirl, "Neil's looking for you, and he doesn't look happy. I'd get a move on to his office if I were you, best not to keep him waiting."

"Right," Ruby nodded to Millicent, with her perfectly salon groomed bobbed haircut, her perfect Clarins makeup and perfect Karen Millen outfit. She took a gulp of her coffee before resting it down on the unit, wishing it was something stronger to give her Dutch courage. Normally, she'd take it in with her, Neil was fairly informal, but she knew she was in for a rocket, so thought it better to leave it and try and look professional.

With her back to Millicent, she widened her eyes and gave Sophie a *I'd better go and face the music* look.

As she made her way through the main open plan office, colleagues were starting to arrive clutching their coffees to go – a timely reminder that with her bank balance, she wouldn't be able to afford a branded coffee anytime soon. From now on, she was cutting back on everything

6

apart from breathing to try in some way to make headway into the debts Richie had left. She greeted each of them she passed with a bright smile, suspecting that, in the next few minutes, it would be well and truly wiped off her face.

The heavily embossed Chief Editor sign on her boss's door felt like it was taunting her as she approached it. She barely noticed it usually, but the tightness in her tummy made it somehow seem bolder. Neil's office was glass, so visible to them all. She'd been on the receiving end of his wrath more times than she cared to think about. It was okay for the tutors at uni to imply journalism would open the door to seeing the world, interacting with influential people and getting the best, headlining stories, but nobody mentioned crap assignments, crap money, and a crap boss.

"Sit," Neil spat, which she promptly did on the seat opposite his desk. It felt like she'd been sent to the headmaster's office to receive her punishment.

She was in deep trouble – but when was she not with him?

2.

"I cannot believe what you did!" Neil's face was puce with anger, "You utterly humiliated him."

Ruby fiddled with her jacket, pulling it together, "I'm sorry if I've . . ."

"Sorry?" he barked, "You think it's acceptable as a reporter representing *this* newspaper to slap a man across his face in full view of everyone in a restaurant. And not only that, you pushed him off his bloody chair. He could have been injured!"

"Yeah, well it was just a shove. How was I to know he'd fall off his chair?"

"It must have been one hell of a shove. You shouldn't have hit him in the first bloody place. What the hell were you thinking?"

"That he was a pervert."

"You were on a job, Ruby . . . you know, the one that pays your salary. He's already been on the phone this morning. As a result of your reckless actions, we are now going to have to pay the cost of his hotel, his food, and his bloody dry cleaning. So, at this moment in time, we have a completely unnecessary expense and no bleeding interview . . . because of you!"

"Hang on a minute," she glared, "shouldn't you be defending me? Don't you have a duty of care to make

8

sure, as my employer, that I'm not pawed over by a dirty old man?"

"For Christ's sake, how old are you? You were working and should have been professional. Slapping a man in public is absolutely unacceptable behaviour and certainly not in a place like the Shard. Because of your stupidity, we've waved goodbye to an interview. And let me remind you how a newspaper works . . . we get interviews, print them, and sell newspapers accordingly. That's what pays all of our salaries. It's not a difficult concept to understand, Ruby. The way you're carrying on, you'll end up shutting the bloody place down."

"Look, I can see you're not happy, and I sort of get that. But sending me to meet with a bloke who thinks reaching for my hand and placing it on the bulge in his pants is not exactly my idea of dinner etiquette."

"Oh, grow up, Ruby. You're not fifteen. You should be able to handle any situation, that's what reporters do. Do you think Millicent got where she is today by slapping every man that made a pass at her?"

She sighed heavily, she didn't owe him anything. Peter Huxley was a lecherous old git. Who cares if she didn't get the lowdown on him winning his libel case. Neil might pay her salary, but he was just like the rest of them. He thought it was quite acceptable to dangle her in front of any bloke to try and get what he was after, only for loose knickers Millicent or one of the other senior reporters to get all the glory writing the story and it going into print with their name on it. Not once has any reference been given to her name in the credits when she'd done all the ground work.

"I tell you what," she glared, "stop sending me on these interviews. Why do I always have to be the one meeting lecherous old men?"

"Why the hell do you think? Don't be so bloody naive. Have you looked in the mirror lately? I'm far more likely to get an interview or information I want by sending you."

"Yeah, well that isn't right. I should be allowed to write up the stories, I'm always sidelined yet I do all the legwork."

"Because that's how it works. Don't you think Millicent or Frank had to start with junior stuff before they moved onto a senior reporter's role?"

She shrugged; of course she knew that was how it all worked. "So, what you're really saying is that I should have groped his bulge, is that it?"

Neil huffed. "I mean it, Ruby, I've had more than enough of your antics, this has to bloody stop."

"Hang on. Anyone would think I mess up regularly the way you're going on."

"Well, your track record isn't exactly brilliant, is it?" he barked. "You made an enemy out of Gordon Sym, he used to give us regular interviews, but not anymore. Not after *you* went to interview him. Funny that," his nostrils flared.

"Yeah, he was another lech, intimating he'd give me the interview if I went to bed with him. All I did was tell him why I wouldn't."

"And you think telling him you couldn't face his bad breath and body odour was the right approach, do you?" he glared. "I think you take some perverse pleasure in knocking these men back."

He was spot on. She hated men expecting sex from her. Her beautiful mother had told her as soon as she went through puberty that she'd pay a price for having luscious curly red hair and huge green eyes – it would lure men in, mainly the unscrupulous ones that were only interested in sex. And she'd been right. But her mother would know more than anyone, she'd been Miss Ireland and Miss Great Britain, always involved in beauty pageants as a young woman, which meant that men thought she was fair game. And so it seems, men thought she was too. Her mother had an expression she used when she'd complain about being on the receiving end of unwanted male attention, she called them OT's – opportunistic tossers, which Ruby always found amusing.

Her silence forced Neil to carry on. "I sincerely hope you do better with this next job," he scowled over the rim of his designer glasses, "call it a *redeem yourself* job. And I'm telling you now, Ruby you owe this newspaper big time."

She sighed. She knew what was coming next. It would be some sort of dire job involving blokes . . . they always were.

"As long as it's not another job sucking up to a dirty old man. I might need to work," and boy did she need it, remembering the email from her bank saying she needed to come in and discuss her overdraft, "but not that badly."

"Nobody expects you to suck up to men, all we ask at the newspaper is that you're professional and treat potential client interviews with respect. That's not too difficult, is it?"

"You'd better define respect, because I'm telling you now, I'm not sleeping with anyone if that's what you think."

"And I've never asked you to sleep with anyone," his intense eyes narrowed, "well, not with a client anyway."

A flush crept up her neck, knowing exactly what he was thinking. He'd tried many times to get her into bed, and not once had he succeeded. More recently though, he'd stopped trying, as if he'd accepted defeat, which she was relieved about. Casual sex had never been for her, in fact, she didn't really like sex. Even with Richie, she'd cared about him and missed him, but not the rubbish sex.

"Go on then," she said quickly, trying to move the conversation on, "what's the job?"

"Hang on a minute. Sophie tells me you have a novel you've written and you're thinking of independently publishing it."

"Yeah," she shrugged thinking of the manuscript on her laptop, the escapism story that kept her going each night sat in her flat with the obligatory glass of wine, "that's right." Why had Sophie told him that? It was her private world where she imagined bringing out her debut novel and it becoming a best-seller earning her millions so she could pay off all her debts, buy her own house and be able to flick through a holiday brochure and go anywhere she fancied without worrying about the cost. "It's not finished though . . . er, I'm at the editing stage," which roughly translated meant she'd only written fifteen chapters. "So, what has that got to do with anything?"

"Well," he cleared his throat as if he was about to offer her the jackpot of jobs when in fact it would be something quite the opposite – a crap job like they always were. "How would you feel about spending some time at a writer's retreat? You'd get an opportunity to attend the lectures and maybe it would help to fine-tune your manuscript. How does that sound?"

"Fishy."

"Why are you always so bloody suspicious?"

"Maybe because every job you ask me to do is a bum job."

"That is not true."

"Tell me one decent job then." She waited for his answer but he couldn't recall one because he knew she was right.

"See, all bum ones."

He sighed. "This job will be mutually beneficial. I'm offering you an opportunity to spend a few days with like-minded people at a writer's retreat." Something was distinctly off; Neil didn't do helping good causes. "You can thank me later," he said, "I would have thought you'd snap my hand off. And I've been thinking," oh, God no, not him thinking, "maybe when you get back, we could try and get you a publisher for your novel and help with sales by featuring extracts in the paper."

Hmm, even fishier.

"I suppose that sounds great from my perspective," she answered, "so what's in it for you, or the newspaper?"

He leaned back in his chair. "You know Sophie has said from the beginning that her baby's father is Edward De'Ath?"

"Yeah, Edward J De'Ath, the multi-millionaire best-selling author." She never understood why he'd use his surname on the front of his books – to her he was Edward Death. An apostrophe didn't change that as far as she was concerned.

"Yep, the very one. But she can't prove that the child is his from a one-night stand and has no DNA to establish that, hence why we can't run the story, much as we want to. We would need to somehow be able to prove categorically he is the father and then the floodgates will open and we'll have an exclusive. Currently, De'Ath won't comment when we've tried to make contact. It's with solicitors, but no further than that."

"Yeah, Sophie was only just saying that it will be costly for her to take him on. She doesn't have that sort of money."

"Absolutely, she can't afford to. But there is a massive exclusive for the paper if we could prove he was Lilly's father."

"Prove? Of course he's Lilly's father, Sophie wouldn't lie."

"Keep your voice down. Nobody is saying that. It's just that Sophie could have had other sexual encounters around the same time for all we know. We can't write an article if he isn't the father. We need to be absolutely certain."

"Well, it sounds like it's going to be a long job then, trying to prove it, if ever."

"Not necessarily. There might be a way to obtain his DNA and prove that De'Ath is Lilly's father."

"What sort of way?" she asked hesitantly.

"It's a bit of a long shot, but one I think is worth taking."

She focussed on him intensely. Whatever was coming next, it would have her name on it.

"He's going to be attending the summer writers' school in Derbyshire, in fact he's a guest lecturer and running a workshop for four days."

"What, this writer's retreat you mentioned?"

"That's right."

"But I thought he lived in the US."

"He does, and God knows what pull the school have, but he's definitely on the programme. Here, look."

She glanced down at the flyer he handed her which was a photocopy of an article announcing that renowned author, Edward J De'Ath will be at the summer school running a four day workshop on novel writing. There was a photograph of him which surprised her. She'd imagined him older somehow, but then remembered that people often used old photos on social media to appear younger and current.

She frowned, "You've lost me. Where do I fit in?"

"I want you to go there and obtain something we can send off for DNA testing so we can prove he's Lilly's father."

"What!? You're kidding me? Even if I got to meet the bloke, how am I going to get a sample of his DNA? What the hell are you expecting me to do?" Images flashed through her mind of a drama she'd watched on Netflix, of a woman extracting semen from a used condom.

She shuddered.

"Nothing like you're imagining," Neil said.

"Thank God for that. What then? Because I have to say, Neil, you're losing me here completely. I know very little about DNA but what I do know is, it has to be something personal like a saliva sample, or hairs etc., and with the best will in the world, I hardly think he's going to open his mouth for some random woman to shove a swab in his gob, or let me cut his hair, do you?"

"Now you're being ridiculous. I'm thinking more along the lines of you *covertly* obtaining some DNA."

"How?"

"By getting into his room and taking some."

"You're having a laugh, surely? How the hell would I get into his room? And even if I did, what are you expecting me to collect exactly?"

"A used tissue, some hairs from his comb, or maybe best of all, his toothbrush. Anything we can send for testing. We just need that one little piece."

She shook her head. "You are seriously losing it. Can you even use DNA obtained in a covert way?"

"We don't need to use it. We just want proof before we go after him. There's no point in exposing him if he isn't the father, this way, once we have proof, we'll pursue him. We don't need to mention we've obtained any DNA at this stage."

"Honestly Neil, this is bordering on preposterous. Please don't tell me Sophie's happy about this."

"Ah, well, here's the thing, she's not going to know – not yet anyway. If we get the sample tested and it proves conclusively he's Lilly's father, then we'll expose De'Ath. But if it's negative, we won't pursue it any further. And the added bonus is, you get help with your writing. What's not to like?"

"Lots!" She got to her feet, "I'm telling you now, this isn't happening. I-am-not-doing-it. Full stop. And if that costs me my job, then so be it."

"This is your last chance, Ruby," his glare demonstrated his authority, "and if you don't comply, it *will* cost you your job."

He didn't try to stop her as she walked out of his office and slammed the door behind her. As she made her way towards her desk, all she could think was how much she needed every penny of her salary to pay off her debts. She couldn't afford to lose her job. But there wasn't a snowball's chance in hell she would contemplate doing what Neil was suggesting. It was completely ridiculous.

This time she was determined to dig her heels in.

As far as she was concerned, he could go and take a running bloody jump.

3.

Edward De'Ath cursed as the black Focus Zetec straddled his lane on the M1 and cut him up. It always irritated him, even though he was used to it. Drivers, particularly young blokes, didn't like flash cars, so the Range Rover Sport he was driving would certainly piss the wannabe Max Verstappens off big time. They seemed to take great delight in overtaking him, as if by doing so, their car was somehow superior. Motoring was his passion and an indulgence that couldn't be hidden. Pretentious wasn't really him, in spite of being able to eat in the finest restaurants, stop at the best hotels, and his home being in the prestigious Upper East side of New York overlooking Central Park, however, extravagances such as luxury motors undoubtedly labelled him as flashy to some.

Increasing the pressure on the accelerator, the power of the three-litre petrol engine excited him. The Range Rover was quite a beauty for a hire car. He owned a couple of classics at home in New York which he loved to thrash along the Storm King Highway, west of the Hudson River. Since being a small boy, the sound of a V8 engine was music to his ears and he used to dream of owning one. So, when his debut novel seven years earlier had become a best-seller in the US and UK, the first thing he purchased was a 1974 carmine red Triumph

Stag. As far as he was concerned, he'd earned it with all the blood, sweat and edits that went into writing a novel that had taken him a number of years to complete. And then, like many new authors, he had to fit writing around paid employment. Now though, he was free to write at his leisure. Yes, he had deadlines like any author, but selling the amount of books he did and regularly topping the best seller lists in both sides of the Atlantic, gave him significant leeway with his agent, publisher and editor.

He glanced at the satnav – less than thirty minutes and he'd be at the writers' school. He was actually looking forward to it despite not having done any lecturing in the UK since Laura, his wife had died. His gut clenched even now at the pain of losing her, even though it was coming up to four years. It never left him. Life was empty without her. Writing was solitary enough without living alone. His home was huge with just him in it. And quiet. As the months turned into years, Laura's vibrant existence faded. Photographs were a constant reminder in all the rooms, but her presence had long gone. It had become only his domain. Of course, he had plenty of friends and acquaintances and his wayward brother, always a thorn in his side, was a constant. He wasn't averse to hooking up with women either, but the only trouble with that was, they were more interested in his bank balance than him. He'd had to break things off with his most recent relationship as she was getting far too domesticated for his liking. None of the women he dated came close to Laura. She had been his future until, for reasons nobody could comprehend, she'd taken her own life. It was a desperate, dreadful time. He persistently berated himself for not seeing any signs of her depression despite family reassuring him there hadn't been any. The passing of time had eased the torment to a certain extent, and work had helped enormously, but at thirty-five, the days were long, and joy and laughter seemed to have departed from his life. In truth, he was lonely.

More recently, in London researching for his next book, a phone call gave him a glimmer of a challenge. His old mucker Garth had called begging for help at a writer's school in Derbyshire. Seemingly one of the lecturers booked as an evening speaker and to undertake some workshops, had cancelled due to ill health and Garth, along with the committee members were frantically trying to find someone. Initially he'd been hesitant, but Garth begged, highlighting the amount of money delegates had paid and how they would be looking forward to the retreat. He'd come up with a few feeble excuses, but his good friend had easily dismissed them, reminding him how much he used to love lecturing, which was why he still did the occasional few in the US. He liked the contrast of imparting storytelling vocally as opposed to watching the words take shape on his PC. The idea of a captive audience with an interest in writing, also appealed. His mate had worn him down and he'd eventually agreed. What harm could it do? He might even enjoy it.

As if Garth knew he was thinking about him, his name came up as a caller on the console. Ed pressed accept and cleared his throat, "Now then, mate."

"Now then, buddy you nearly here?"

Ed glanced at the satnav, "Another twenty minutes or so."

"That's good, I can't wait to introduce you to everyone. You've scored me plenty of scout points. The committee are thrilled to be getting you – it's quite a coup and has improved my kudos no end. They've been scrambling around trying to find someone, anyone who can help out and I've managed to hook you."

"Do you get anything out of it, then?"

"Not really. Well, I say not really, I'm planning to run for deputy chair next year, so it'll get me in the good books, if you'll pardon the pun. I know Jocelyn's delighted you're coming, she's quite a fan."

"Remind again me who Jocelyn is?"

"She's the chair."

"Don't you want to be the chair? Why the deputy?"

"Jocelyn has another year to go so it's not up for grabs yet. The deputy is good though as it gives me a chance to see if it's what I want to do. As I've told you before, I do this retreat once a year; it's great to do something different. And now I've managed to snare you, I'm hoping to shamefully use you to my advantage. So, don't whatever you do say you're not coming back another year. I need to capitalise on this big time."

"I won't be back," he said firmly, "I told you this is a one off."

"I know that and you know that, but no point in telling them that. Let's leave it open, shall we? Let them think I can persuade you to do another year."

Ed laughed, "If it helps you, then I'm happy to. I'm looking forward to catching up. We need to fix up a date for you to come and visit me in the US."

"I'd like that. And there's no reason why I can't now Elise and I are no longer together."

"Yeah, let's get it sorted this week and firm something up."

"Will do. Right, I'll see you when you get here. Now, don't be expecting anything palatial like you're used to, will you?"

"What, you mean there aren't any electronic blinds, a housekeeper turn-down service and chocolates on my pillow at night?"

"Er . . . in a word, no. But you have got curtains, your room is en suite, and I'm sure I could rustle up a Mars bar."

Ed chuckled. "Thank Christ for that. I mean the en suite not the chocolate bar. I'm a bit old to be using bathrooms on the corridor."

"Me too, but we did once upon a time, didn't we? Those were the days, eh?"

Ed remembered only too well the fleapits they'd stayed in on breaks from uni when they'd travel here, there and everywhere, doing any jobs that had living accommodation attached. They'd become experts in kitchen work, bar work and even cleaning hotel rooms.

"Oh, before I forget, you've mentioned to the front desk and the housekeepers about my privacy?"

"Yep, all sorted. No one is going to get within fifty feet of your room . . . unless you want them to, of course."

"No, I most definitely don't."

"I don't know what you think this place is," Garth sniggered, "but as big a hit as you are with the ladies, you'll not find any here naked and waiting patiently in your bed for you."

"You might well laugh; I've had it more than once in hotels. One woman was so drunk, I had to stop in a different room that night as they couldn't shift her. I had a hell of a job making them believe she wasn't with me."

"Lucky you, but I can assure you that you'll not have that problem here," Garth's amusement was evident in his voice, "the delegates are more interested in the written word than any extracurricular activities you could provide."

"I'm delighted to hear it," Ed grinned to himself. "Seriously though, I do value my privacy, so thanks for doing that. I'll be there shortly. Where do I find you after I've checked in? I've got the instructions for getting to my room in the bumf they sent. It seems I don't go to reception."

"No, you don't. You head for your accommodation block, they have greeters there. When you've offloaded, come to the bar, it's the main thoroughfare of the place, you'll see it signposted. I'll be in there. The first drink's on me."

"That's good to hear, in that case, mine's a pint of whisky."

Garth chuckled. "See you shortly."

Light of heart, Ed exited the motorway via junction 28, heading towards Derby, strangely pleased he'd agreed to attend. A few days doing something completely different felt almost invigorating. No writing deadlines, solitary dinners staring at an empty wine bottle, just a few days imparting his knowledge with like-minded people interested in the written word, which was his passion. It might work out well after all.

A stress-free week prior to returning to the States.

Just what he needed.

4.

With the sun blazing on the Toyota hire car, Ruby pulled the visor down, grumbling inwardly at tight git Neil, her boss, who wouldn't pay for a more luxurious car. Basic he'd said, and basic she'd got. Thankfully there was a sun roof, which was open and she'd cracked both front windows so a breeze was cooling the car. With the radio on low, she was barely listening to the rubbish, until a slow melodic song jogged a painful memory. It was the song her and Richie had danced to at her friend's wedding. It had been in the early stages of their relationship when they were beginning to explore their mutual attraction and still discovering each other. Obviously she hadn't discovered enough as he'd taken her for a complete fool. Wormed his way into her life until he was living in her flat for most of the week, and the days he wasn't, he was away working in his job as a salesman. Well, that was the yarn he'd spun her – which was code for his other life, the one where he had another girlfriend who'd suffered the same fate as her. Both completely fleeced by him.

Bastard.

If she didn't have all the debt Richie had left her with, she wouldn't be on her way to the latest crap job Neil had assigned her, despite her protests. Although the words *written warning* hadn't been used by him, Millicent

26

magnificent hadn't shied away from them. And Neil had said this job was her last chance. She had no choice. If she didn't deliver on this job, it was highly likely she'd be looking for another one with a none too glowing reference from Neil. Or *bloody* Neil as her and Sophie called him. He seemed to use the word constantly. They'd joke that surely as a journalist he should have a more extensive vocabulary to call on.

She reached for her bottle of water. If she couldn't get the specimen for DNA testing, and ended up losing her job, she might have to consider joining her parents in Sydney for a year or two. They were desperate for her to emigrate, but right now, there wasn't a chance. She had to clear, or maybe reduce some of the debt Richie had left her with. She wasn't stupid, far from it, it was just that he'd been terribly convincing, the perfect boyfriend more or less. Everything had been good between them, they had similar tastes – both loved theatre, comedy clubs and Italian food, almost a perfect match although perhaps not in the bedroom. Despite caring deeply for him, she hadn't been struck by the sex. She wasn't widely experienced, she could count the amount of relationships she'd had on one hand, or maybe even three fingers, and each of them had been unsatisfactory for her. According to Cosmopolitan, every woman should be having sex on a daily basis, if not twice. Who were these twice a day women? That was never going to be her. Faking it became the norm and Richie barely seemed to notice. Or if he did, he never complained. It certainly hadn't held him back, that was for sure. But she'd been happy to comply, she cared for him and that's what mattered she told herself.

The signs were becoming more frequent indicating she was close to The Conference Centre, where the writer's retreat was being held. Eventually the chequered flag appeared on the satnav and an American accent told her she had reached her destination. She veered of the main carriageway and onto a narrow road following the arrows directing towards the reception area further down. It was nice to see the grazing cows in the adjacent field – it gave a feeling of calmness, quite the opposite to the hustle and bustle of London.

She spotted a sign indicating Lakeside Plus which was where she'd been allocated to stay. The road took her around the back of a building with beige coloured uniform bricks and casement windows, housing endless dormitory rooms by the look of it. But it was the secluded lake to the right which held her attention and caused her to slow down, apply the handbrake and cut the engine. It looked stunning, baked in the warm sunshine and surrounded by willow trees and shrubbery of all colours. No doubt a place for quiet contemplation or maybe to exercise around. She'd brought her gym kit with her intending to do some running while she was there. The lake area looked perfect for just that. She certainly wasn't going to attend loads of lectures; she'd had enough of those at university. There were one or two on the programme that held her interest, and hopefully would help with her own novel, but she intended to relax a little too. After all, it was almost a holiday. One week away from the office was perfect. She was determined to enjoy some alone time to forget about her dire financial situation which would be there soon enough when she returned to London.

She turned on the ignition, put the car in gear and set off, turning left again past the lake and continued towards the sign for Lakeside Plus. The beige brick and uniform small windows reminded her of uni. As she reached the far end, she turned right onto an elevated part of the car park which, judging by the white lines, looked to be able to accommodate about fourteen cars. Her failure to apply more pressure on the accelerator to move up the incline was an indication of her lack of driving of late, and the car engine immediately stalled.

Bugger!

She restarted the car and accelerated up the incline and found a space at the end of the car park, and pulled in. But glancing in her left wing mirror, she could tell she wasn't quite in the white lines, so needed to pull back and straighten up. As she put the car into reverse, her phone, resting on the passenger seat, lit up indicating a text had come through. It wasn't her intention to read the text, but momentarily, keeping one hand on the steering wheel, she lifted the phone and glanced the screen to check who it was. It was Neil – no doubt bursting to give her more *bloody* instructions.

"Bang!" – the car shuddered.

"What the hell!" . . . her heart felt like it had been catapulted out of her chest as her eyes shot to the rearview mirror. All she could see was a huge red car, dwarfing her car. The idiot driver must have been straightening up as she'd been doing, clearly without looking and reversed into her.

"Shit. Shit. Shit." Still clutching her phone, she pushed the car door open and stepped out, as the tall moron in shorts and a red tee shirt was getting out of the red car with his nostrils flaring.

"What the hell do you think you're doing?" he exploded as he made his way forward, his eyes focussed on the rear of his car, compressing her bumper.

"What do you mean, what am I doing?" she snapped, "You reversed into me!" She stared at her car with the crumpled bumper, "Don't you look behind you before you carry out manoeuvres in your car?"

His fists seemed almost clenched as if he was refraining from punching her. "I have a rear view camera for that. And when I began reversing, your car was static. Parked up," he glared, fishing his phone out of his pocket.

"Well, as you can see, it wasn't," she scowled; furious he was taking no notice of her. He was positioning his phone to take a photograph. "And for your information," she continued, "yes, I'm absolutely fine, no injuries at all, thank you for asking."

His deep breath in, smacked of irritation. "It wasn't the sort of a bang that I'd expect you to be injured."

"You could have at least asked."

"Oh, right, do forgive me," he said in a voice laced with sarcasm, "but right now I'm more concerned about the damage. I'll be paying out big time through no fault of my own, and in my experience, these things are always costly."

"And you know that because you bang into cars regularly, do you?"

Who the hell was this pompous prick? Judging by the top-end car, he clearly wasn't short of money, whereas she'd be paying the insurance back until the day she retired. God, more debt.

"No, I don't *bang* into cars regularly. For your information I have a blemish free driving licence, but this is a hire car, therefore I know already it's going to cost me plenty, through no fault of my own."

"It was your fault, you didn't check properly before you reversed and I'm sure our insurance companies will see exactly that."

"Are you serious?" His eyes bulged, "You were static, looking down at something. No doubt your phone, that's what you young people do all the time."

"I was not, and don't patronise me. Mine's a hire car too, so you're not the only one going to be screwed."

"Look," he ran his hand through his thick wavy hair, "arguing like this is getting us nowhere. If you give me your hire car details, I'll give you mine and then we can notify them both. But first of all, you'd better pull into the space you were supposed to be in, and I'll do the same."

"Hang on a minute, I want a photo too." She took a couple of pictures, only because she'd seen him do so and thought she ought to. It wouldn't have occurred to her had she not seen him do it. Without saying another word, she got back into her car, switched on the ignition, and moved forward into the parking space. Her temple throbbed – she was going to be in deep shit with Neil, she'd had to beg him to let her have a hire car on expenses. She glanced back in the mirror at the idiot driver. There was something familiar about him. It felt like she'd met him before, yet she knew she hadn't. Reaching in the glove compartment she located the hire car agreement and stepped out of the car. He appeared to be clutching similar, with his phone in the other hand as he moved towards her. "If you give me your name and address," he said.

"Ruby Lowe. And I'm not giving you my address, you could be anyone. I don't give details out like that to random men I've just met, let alone careless drivers."

"Are you for real?" he snapped. "It would be *most unlikely* I'd be stalking you, now . . . or ever. And as for a careless driver, you want to look in the mirror, lady. This is entirely your fault."

"Is it now? Well, let's see what the insurance companies say. She opened the notes app on her phone, "Can I have your name?"

"Edward De'Ath."

She reeled back . . . surely not? Fate wouldn't be that cruel. It couldn't be him . . . it just couldn't. Disbelievingly, she stared and the more she did, she recognised his familiarity, except he was far more attractive in real life than the photograph she'd seen. And photos don't give an indication of height or presence. She was tall for a female so well used to men being around the same height at her, or in some cases shorter, whereas he towered above her. His appeal was evident despite him needing a shave. Tall, dark and handsome didn't do him justice. No wonder Sophie had slept with him, he'd be pretty hard to resist.

"When you're ready," he said sarcastically as she continued to stare.

"Oh, right, sorry." She quickly typed in his name.

"My car is hired from Hertz at Victoria station, London."

She was taking everything down he said, but how accurately she wasn't sure. In all her thoughts about how she was going to obtain something they could have tested for DNA, she hadn't envisaged banging into him in a car park. It was a complete disaster.

She told him her hire car company details which he made note of. Every bit of her was willing him to go so she could gather herself. Of all the pompous gits in the world, he reverses into her, or she to him as he was accusing. Whatever, the damage was done and not just to the cars. What a ridiculous start. If she wasn't so angry, she could almost laugh. It was like something from a Mills and Boon novel when the male and the female have a car bump and end up falling madly in love. Thank God that wouldn't apply in their case. He might be pretty hot on the eye, but no way did he float her boat. Now, as a result of the incident, getting anything of his for DNA testing was going to be twice as hard. He was hardly likely to be spending any time in her company for the duration of the course. An image flashed through her mind of registering at a Job Centre and paying a hefty sum of money to the hire car company, which she didn't have.

Bloody Neil – she could throttle him.

5.

Eager to get as far away from De'Ath as she could, Ruby swiftly dragged her case along the gravel pathway towards the back entrance to Lakeside Plus. Judging by the racket the wheels were making, one of them must have locked. But purchasing a new case was hardly a priority, especially with her dwindling bank balance. And she was unlikely to be going on any overseas holidays soon.

Manoeuvring her case and laptop through the door, she kept hold of it so it didn't swing on the person coming up behind her. The smile on her face faded when she realised it was him again. Hostile and towering above her, he took hold of the door, and with a deadpan face, grunted a thank you. He well and truly lived up to his godforsaken name. Without the apostrophe, he was Death. Cold and stiff – yeah, that suited him.

A small queue had formed in the foyer in front of two ladies sitting behind a desk giving out envelopes, which must be the key cards and programme an earlier email had indicated would be given out on arrival. As she stood in line, she was acutely aware De'Ath was behind her, no doubt breathing venom down her neck. And just as it was her turn to step forward, he slipped past her to the second woman sitting behind a box of envelopes. In unison they gave their names to the respective servers.

"Sorry," the woman with a lanyard showing her name was Jane said, "I didn't get that."

No, she wouldn't, because of him. Couldn't he have waited just a second?

"Ruby Lowe," she repeated as Jane began to rake through the box in front of her with the named envelopes.

The second woman dealing with De'Ath almost squealed her delight, "Welcome. We're thrilled to have you here, Mr De'Ath; it's so kind of you to step in at short notice," she gushed, "your books arrived from your publisher so they'll be displayed in the book room along with the other authors' books."

"Great," he cleared his throat, "thank you." It was almost as if he was embarrassed about the attention. He must be used to it, surely?

"I'm sure there'll be plenty of delegates eager to get their hands on a signed copy from you. I've read them all and loved every single one of them. Although I prefer a Kindle copy as I don't have a lot of room in my flat for a book case."

Ruby, forced to listen while waiting for her envelope, shuffled from one foot to another while the woman continued fawning over him, "I did love *Raindrops Keep Falling off my Tread,* such a clever title. It sounds almost comedic, but it's nothing like that with the car chase and that massive twist at the end. Brilliant!"

"Here we are, Ruby," Jane handed a pack to her. "There's a lanyard inside the pack, please wear it at all times while you're here." She pointed to the door behind her, "To get to your room, you need to go through the double doors, keep going through the next fire door and you'll find room 314 on the left hand side."

"Thank you." Ruby reached for her case, barely listening as the one-woman De'Ath appreciation society carried on, "I'll look forward to speaking with you sometime during the week."

"That'd be great," she heard him answering as she moved towards the double doors leading to the rooms, pulling her suitcase in one hand and her laptop in the other. A smile twitched at her lips thinking about his unfortunate surname. Edward Death – what a stupid name, and a crime writer too. A more appropriate connotation as far as she was concerned was Death-Ed, or even better, Dead-Ed. Yeah, Dead-Ed, the obnoxious author who can't reverse a car properly.

As she passed along the corridor with the white walls and ply veneer doors, she quickly located room 314. She tore open her pack, pulled out the key card and tapped it on the lock, holding the door open with her foot and reaching for her case. Surreptitiously, her eyes moved to her left, and low and behold, Dead-Ed himself was entering the room directly next door, clearly not looking her way on purpose.

Jesus! – that's all she needed, him as a neighbour. She entered her room and let the swing door slam behind her, blowing out a huge breath of frustration. How the hell had he of all people, ended up in the room next to her? You couldn't make it up.

She surveyed the basic room in front of her. The double bed was made up with white crisp linen, two turquoise cushions were propped against the pillows and there was a matching throw at the bottom of the bed. She peeked at the functional en suite with basic white fixtures. It was hardly the Ritz, but it would do. It was clean which she was relieved about. And there was a kettle and a tray of teas and coffees.

The view from the window was the car park surrounding the building and further afield, there were more cows grazing. She could just about see her hire car below, but didn't dwell on that. It was best to try and forget that episode and concentrate on why she was there. She lifted her case onto the bed and started to unpack, hanging her clothes in the alcove area assigned with coat hangers and a shoe rack, and placing her underwear in the chest of drawers and cosmetics in the bathroom. As she was thinking about the almost impossible task ahead, a thought struck her – a bit of good fortune maybe after the ill-fated car bump. Dead-Ed residing next door to her could prove fortuitous in the long run. Possibly, she might be able to nip into his room while it was being serviced and get what she needed. It might all work out fine now she wasn't going to be spending any time with him as she'd originally intended. Yep, every cloud and all that. Her mood felt lighter until her mobile rang and she saw the caller.

"Hi Neil," she said sounding brighter than she actually felt, "I was just going to ring you."

"Really?" his tone indicated he doubted it.

"Yeah, course."

"You're there then. Hire car okay?"

"Fine," she lied. God, she was really going to be in for it. No sense in alerting him to that now though, if she got the DNA sample, maybe he'd go easy on her. It would after all be a massive scoop for the paper if they got proof Dead-Ed had fathered a child and wouldn't accept responsibility.

"And the room?" he continued, as if he cared.

"Dire. It feels like I'm back at uni, they're pretty basic."

"Yeah, well, you're not on holiday, you are working."

"Don't I know it," she said under her breath.

"Sorry?"

"Nothing. I was just thinking aloud. Actually, I need to get a move on, I think there's some sort of delegates welcome meeting."

"Before you do, remember you're not there for anything else other than why you've been sent. Attend the lectures by all means, it's a means to an end, but don't be getting bloody distracted. I haven't paid nine hundred quid for you to be swanning around. You've got a job to do."

"How could I forget when I've got you keeping tabs on me?"

"Yeah, well, someone has to. Now this is important, have you got a pen handy?"

She moved to the desk and fished one out of the welcome pack, "Yeah, go ahead."

"There's a chairman welcome speech tonight you need to attend."

"How do you know?"

"I just do. Now listen carefully and write this down so you don't make a mistake. When you go into the main hall for the welcome speech, you need to sit on the back row on the last chair next to the centre aisle."

"Why?"

"Have you got that? The back row, the aisle seat. It'll be the row on the right, looking towards the stage."

"Yeah, got that, but why?"

"Because they're having a raffle and that seat will have the winning ticket."

"Winning ticket for what?"

"A ticket that will help you get what we need, so make sure you sit in that particular seat."

"What if someone's already sitting in it?"

"There will be initially, but he'll get up and move forward as he sees you approaching. You need to take the seat."

"This is all sounding ridiculous Neil, why won't you tell me? What exactly is this *winning ticket* for? I might not even want it. And who the hell knows I'm here for God's sake? That's the last thing I want, this is all starting to sound like a complete farce."

"Ruby . . ." he emphasised her name, "for once in your life, just do as you're told. Take the bloody seat like I'm telling you."

"Okay, okay, but don't be going on at me if I can't. There must be loads of people here. It's not going to be easy picking out a particular seat."

"Will you stop finding problems where there aren't any. All will become apparent when you win. The element of surprise will be more normal if you don't know. It's going to help us achieve our objectives, I can assure you."

She sighed. To her, it was all sounding like a cheap TV comedy. But she was too tired to argue with him, her jaw and neck were throbbing from the car bump with Dead-Ed. And it was best to keep on Neil's good side, she'd be feeling his wrath soon enough about the damage to the hire car.

"Alright, I hear you. Look, I really need to be getting a move on."

"Right, well don't forget why you're there. Get making De'Ath's acquaintance as soon as you can. I've fixed it so you will anyway. You only have six nights to get what we need. We must have something so we can do the DNA test. Have you got that?"

Yeah, yeah, yeah. I've got all of that as well as very shortly, a bill from the hire car company.

"Got it, boss."

"And keep me posted. I want to know as soon as you've got the sample. Then you can get the hell out of there. The last thing we want is De'Ath getting suspicious."

"Okay, will do, bye for now." She ended the call. If he thought she was going to be giving him a daily bulletin,

41

he could think again. Her intention now was to somehow get in Dead-Ed's room for his toothbrush, or failing that, a glass he'd been drinking out of. And then she was out of there. If it wasn't an adequate enough sample to obtain DNA . . . so what? She'd have done her bit. At the end of the day, she'd complied so he couldn't give her a written warning at Millicent had inferred.

She headed for the shower with one thing on her mind. Sneaking next door in Dead-Ed's room for the toothbrush was the best option. The thought of sitting down in his company waiting to pinch his glass, made her shudder. It'd be a tall order to orchestrate sitting with him for a drink now anyway, and more so because she disliked the man, not only for pranging her car, but for rejecting his own child. Shows the sort of man he was. Unprincipled. He deserved exposing for exactly who he was. People might not be as keen to buy his books and gush over him like the greeter was earlier.

The shower water cascaded over her, running onto her neck and back. She savoured the warm water, hoping it would ease some of the muscle tension. Her thoughts drifted back to Neil. It was unlike him to be evasive. She was more used to him being direct and in her face.

What the hell was this winning ticket prize going to be?

6.

"I'm telling you, straight into the back of me," Ed was sitting in the lively lounge area alongside Garth, "she has no idea how near death she was, I could have strangled the stupid woman. And then, she had the audacity to tell me it was my fault and that I'd reversed into her."

"Sounds like six of one and half a dozen of the other to me," Garth shrugged.

"Cheers mate." Ed took a gulp of his pint, "Glad to have you in my corner."

"I'm just saying, by the sound of things you both reversed at the same time and were unlucky. Anyway," Garth frowned, "did you say it's a Range Rover you've hired? Surely it's got reverse sensors, hasn't it?"

"Yeah," Ed wiped some froth off his mouth and pulled a face, "it just all happened so fast."

"Right," Garth said, his tone heavy in an *it serves you right,* sort of way.

"I know, I know. Let's shut up about it for now, shall we. I'll deal with it later."

Ed's eyes drifted around the room. It was filling up and the noise level was rising with chatter. Despite several coffee machines scattered around, a queue was forming at the bar. The space was large enough to accommodate plenty of delegates and the furniture was positioned well for socialising. The main area around the bar was split into quadrants with large comfy sofas positioned squarely in each of the corners, with coffee tables set in the middle of the squares. Smaller occasional tables with stools ran down the centre of the huge lounge area, and moving towards the library and main reception, there were more tables and chairs and the whole area had a huge wrap around conservatory, all perfect for interacting and chatting.

"It's a great place for this sort of event," Ed said, "I like the way it's all set out. How many delegates are you expecting?"

"Two hundred and twelve I believe," Garth said, "Yeah, it's great for conferences and large groups, the classrooms are typical and the hall pretty basic, but it all works. There's been a saying amongst delegates for long enough that when you come here; you're touched by the magic dust. It's quite sweet I think and certainly a special place."

"I can see that. The rooms are pretty basic, though," Ed said.

"Yep, I did warn you," Garth said, turning to look at a woman approaching. "Ah, here's Jocelyn now." He stood up as an attractive blonde arrived, and Ed did too.

"Hi, Jocelyn, this is Edward De'Ath."

Ed reached out his hand, "Pleased to meet you, Jocelyn."

"You too," she shook his hand. "You got here, then, I was rather worried you wouldn't."

She was a petite lady, mid to late forties, wearing what looked like a designer jacket in navy blue and a checked skirt which flattered her, especially with the huge killer heels. Plenty of slap tastefully applied to her face, but any attractiveness was destroyed by false eyelashes that looked like two awnings extending from her eyelids.

"No problem, it was easy enough to find."

"Can I get you a drink while you chat to Ed?" Garth asked.

"I wouldn't mind a soft drink before I speak, maybe a lime and soda." She turned to Ed, "I've got the welcome speech to give in half an hour."

"Another for you, mate?" Garth asked.

"I'm fine for now, thanks."

"Okay," I'll be right back."

"Please . . . take a seat," Jocelyn said, sitting herself next to him, her skirt hitching up to display a shapely set of pins. She seemed like a confident woman, attractive with her hair cropped short in an impish style. It suited her.

"I'm so grateful you stepped in at the last minute, I honestly don't know what we'd have done if you hadn't."

"I'm sure you'd have found someone."

"I doubt that."

"Well, the pleasure's all mine, I can assure you. I was kicking my heels anyway before returning to the US."

"Ah, yes, Garth said you lived in America. New York, isn't it?"

"It is."

"But you aren't American, not with that accent," she smiled, her heavily made-up eyes looking directly into his. Surely she wasn't flirting already – maybe he was imagining it? Or possibly the beer was of a higher gravity than he was used to.

"No, I'm British. My wife was American."

"Ah, yes, Garth did say."

"Where are you from?" he asked, keen to move the conversation on. He never liked to vocalise that his precious Laura was dead.

"York."

"Ah, beautiful historic York, a lovely city."

"I think so, although it can get rather lonely. I lost my husband two years ago and I find that I don't get invited to as many gatherings, dinners etc., as I used to. It's as if, as a single woman," she arched her brows, "I might be on the prowl." It was there again, her vivid blue eyes finding his, almost like she was giving out the message she was available. Fortunately Garth returning prevented him having to respond. As his gaze strayed past his friend and focussed on the bar, the one person he was determined to give a wide berth to was being served. Ruby redhead. Inexplicably, his heartrate thumped, which was alien to him and only confirmed his earlier thoughts that the *Old Peculiar* bitter was particularly strong and his beer goggles were firmly in place. It couldn't possibly be anything to do with her. But, he had to admit, even dressed casually, she certainly was striking. Her thick mane of red curly hair flowing down her back made her look like she belonged on the set of a Poldark drama, riding a horse bareback across the cliffs. Since the car park incident, she'd changed her clothes and looked quite hot in a pair of tight denim jeans that looked like they'd been painted on her long, lean legs, and wearing a cute white tee shirt with a logo he couldn't quite read from the distance he was sitting.

But he knew exactly what it ought to say . . . Drivers beware – I should be riding a bike.

Or maybe just a big red L plate would be more fitting.

Ed chuckled to himself, admiring her arse as she turned to the bar to get served.

"You okay?" he heard Garth say. "You look miles away."

"I'm good." He knocked back the rest of his beer. "I think I will have another pint."

7.

With her white lanyard around her neck indicating she was a first-time attendee, and clutching her gin and tonic from the bar, Ruby approached a seating area where there appeared to be a spare seat well away from Dead-Ed who she'd spotted talking to another bloke. She wasn't by any means searching for him, quite the opposite – it was more by accident their eyes met across the lounge. And he was as quick as she to look away. He couldn't have been clearer he didn't want to engage. Good!

The place was buzzing with chatter as people greeted each other, clearly some old friends getting reacquainted, and there seemed to be a range of ages with women outnumbering the men.

"Is this seat taken?" she asked a girl who appeared to be of a similar age, with vibrant black hair cut in a bob style. Her cute blue paisley dress and white pumps made Ruby wish she'd made more of an effort, and she could have done – she'd brought enough stuff with her to rival Primark. She hadn't been entirely sure what people wore at a summer school. Looking around, there seemed to be a mixture of some making quite an effort, while others were more casual.

"It's yours," the girl smiled; she was wearing a white lanyard also.

Ruby sat down and rested her drink on the table. "Thank you. There aren't many seats left."

Even standing room was sparse; the place was filling up by the minute and the overflow was seated outside at the tables by the lawn area.

"No, there aren't," the girl said. She was pretty, with huge brown eyes and lovely lengthy curled eyelashes. "I'm Verity. It's my first time here, what about you?"

Ruby held up her lanyard, "Yeah, me too, I'm Ruby. It's certainly busy, I don't know what I thought but I hadn't imagined there'd be so many here. Have you come far?"

"Nottingham, what about you?"

"London."

"Gosh, that's quite a way, aren't there any writing retreats any closer to you?"

"Yeah, plenty, but this one has a good reputation."

"Oh, it does. Do you write already?" Verity took a sip of what looked like Coke, "I mean have you had anything published?"

"No, not yet, but I'm hoping. What about you?"

"I've got a couple of books on Amazon."

"Really? You must be quite a competent writer already then, what's brought you here?"

"To improve really. I'd like to secure a traditional publishing deal, or even an agent," she shrugged, as if that was completely improbable, "this is a great writing school for helping with those intro letters, writing blurbs and a synopsis, so I've heard, anyway."

"Excuse me," a stocky man, with a short, almost shaved head leaned in and reached for some empty glasses from the table in front of them. "Welcome, ladies," he said, his eyes focussing on Ruby's lanyard. He looked like a bouncer of some sort with an earring in his right ear and his short-sleeved white shirt displaying heavily tattooed arms. Why wasn't he scrutinising Verity's badge quite the way he was hers? Or was he checking out her boobs?

"Thank you," Ruby said, feeling her cheeks warming. She waited until he left before continuing the conversation. "Carry on . . . you were saying you've written two books. You must be pretty good to already have them published."

"Self-published. I'm one of those independent authors. I like to think they're okay, there's always room for improvement though." Verity curled one side of her hair behind her ear, "Thing is, anyone can upload a book. Plenty of people do and they aren't that good. You know, poor spelling and grammar. Not to mention weak storylines and glaring plot holes. Many don't engage the services of an editor and just upload what they've written."

"That must give independent authors a bad name I would have thought?"

"Yeah, it does. But that said, there are some fabulous independent authors. I always go for those when I'm after a new book, it's great to support them rather than the ones signed to the big publishers. What about you?"

Ruby didn't read much at all, if she did, it was more often a chick lit paperback she'd grabbed in a supermarket. "All sorts really, but now you've said that, I will try and read more independent authors."

"Have you got a Kindle?"

"Yeah," Ruby said thinking of the one her mother had bought her the previous Christmas which was shoved in a drawer somewhere. Or maybe Richie had taken it to sell for all she knew? "I tend to read paperbacks though."

"Yeah, me too. But they're getting expensive whereas electronic books are so cheap."

"That's true." And certainly something she'd have to think about because paperback books were not something she'd be buying for a while with her debts.

"What about your own writing?" Verity asked, "Where are you with it?"

Ruby blew out a breath, "Still learning really." She reached for her drink feeling almost like she should be crossing her fingers behind her back for telling lies. "I've written my first novel," at least that bit was partly true.

"That's good. What genre is it?"

"Crime." Ruby was keen to expand and appear more convincing, "It's called *Big Mistake*, but that's only a working title, it might change after this week. That's why I've come really, to try and learn a bit more and improve it. It's all pretty new to me."

"Yeah, it is hard when you first start, but I'm sure this week will help." Verity's eyes looked past Ruby towards the double exit doors. "It looks like people are making their way into the hall for the welcome address from the chair. Shall we go together . . . unless you're meeting someone?"

"No, not at all, I'm here on my own. That'd be nice. What about our drinks?" Ruby had barely touched hers.

The lady sitting next to them interjected, "You can take them with you, it's quite informal in the hall."

"Great," Ruby reached for her glass, "I'll follow you then as I'm not sure exactly where I'm going."

"Me neither," Verity said, pulling the programme out of her bag.

"We're heading that way," the same woman said, wearing a yellow lanyard that according to the programme, indicated a more than once attendee, "follow us."

They headed out of the lounge and into the grounds towards the main hall. Ruby's task now had to somehow negotiate this so-called winning seat. Part of her wanted to ignore it completely, but Neil did pay her salary. And, at the end of the day, whatever this winning ticket was, it couldn't be anything too onerous. It might somehow help. She wasn't sure how, but thought she ought to go along with it.

The afternoon sun was still shining as they made their way outside with several others for the short walk to the hall, passing the outdoor tables and chairs situated on the grass. "Here we are," Verity stopped walking as they stood at the double doors with a *Main Hall* sign, "this is it."

Ruby followed Verity through the double doors and once inside, quickly glanced at the rows of chairs lined up facing the small stage with a large screen towering above it. There were other smaller screens around the hall for those sitting further back. Her eyes darted frantically around the hall trying to locate the exact chair Neil had instructed her to sit on.

"Where do you fancy sitting?" Verity asked, "somewhere in the middle?"

It quickly became apparent to Ruby where she should be sitting. The bloke collecting the used glasses earlier in the bar area, was unmistakably the plant. So he had been checking out her lanyard and not her boobs – or maybe both, she thought, remembering his stare and blushing again.

"How about the back row?" Ruby said casually as she moved closer towards him, her gaze purposely roaming around the room in an undecided sort of way. The guy stood up as they got near to him, "You can have this seat if you want."

"Thank you," she nodded, positioning herself directly next to the spare chair, "if you're sure?"

"I am. I think I'd be better nearer the front," he said and strode off down the aisle. Ruby had to think quickly – there was only one seat, and she would appear rude if she sat down and dismissed Verity. She faked an apologetic smile to the middle-aged lady sitting in the adjacent seat, "I know it's a bit like we're back at school, but would you mind moving along so my friend and I can sit together?" The woman's face was set as she begrudgingly nudged her mate, and they hitched themselves along the row leaving two spare seats. Ruby moved aside to let Verity pass to take one of them.

"You go ahead," Verity said, "I'm okay sitting at the end."

No, no, no. That was the winning seat. Ruby had to have it.

"Would you mind if I take the aisle one," she pulled a face," it's my long legs; I get cramp if I can't stretch them out."

"Oh, sure," Verity said, moving past and sitting down, "I wish I had that problem."

Ruby breathed out an exhausted sigh of relief as she sat down on the aisle seat. She'd only been at the writers' school for a couple of hours and already she was shattered. What a palaver of a day – smashing into Dead-Ed's car and now waiting to win whatever stupid prize was on offer. She savoured a huge gulp of the sharp gin and tonic and placed the glass underneath her chair. The hall was filling up and her gaze strayed towards the man who'd been the plant taking a seat closer to the front. Who on earth was he? And what was she going to win? She couldn't fathom it out. But it had better bloody well help her get what she came for, 'cause she'd well and truly had enough already.

8.

An attractive woman with an impish haircut stood at the lectern. "Good afternoon, everybody and welcome. For those of you that don't know me, I'm Jocelyn Moore, chair of the summer writers' school. I won't keep you long, I just want to go through a few essentials."

The PowerPoint presentation kicked in and Jocelyn ran through a few housekeeping rules before explaining the evening for the first timers, or white badgers as they were referred to. Seemingly they were to sit at the tables allocated for dinner that particular evening, with a regular summer school ambassador assigned to it. It was a great opportunity for any questions and to meet other new delegates. After the first evening, there would be no prearranged seating.

Jocelyn then ran through the evening speakers and a photograph appeared on the screen of each of them, including Dead-Ed. She gushed about how fortunate the school was to have the legendary writer, Edward De'Ath step in at the last minute to be a guest speaker and run a workshop. Ruby shuffled in her seat. If they only knew how *the legend* had fathered a child and was totally ignoring his responsibilities. He was far removed from the goody-two-shoes everyone thought he was.

Jocelyn continued, "I'd like to take this opportunity to thank Green Meadow for hosting the summer school. As many that are returning know, it's an excellent venue. I'm sure you'll all be comfortable while you're here. Can I ask Mr Daryl Hill, the manager, to come up to introduce himself?"

The *bouncer* who'd been checking out her lanyard and saved her seat stepped onto the stage and took the mic from Jocelyn. The manager no less. Ruby wasn't sure she felt relief or trepidation, knowing he was involved. There was something about him she didn't like yet she'd not had anything to do with him. More of a sixth sense he could be trouble.

"Welcome everyone. I'm Daryl Hill, the manager, as Jocelyn has already said. I have an office at the front of reception if anyone has any queries. Please don't leave any issues to fester, if there is something not quite right, let us know. If I'm not on duty, there is always a deputy but I'm likely to be here for the week. And we have a night manager too, so anything, however small, please speak up. It's important to us that you are happy and comfortable while you're here. I'd hate to hear when you've gone home on any evaluations that things hadn't been right. So . . . do have a great week all of you, thank you."

He stepped down from the stage to a round of applause.

"Thank you, Daryl," Jocelyn smiled as he walked down the aisle. His eyes met Ruby's as he walked past. She quickly looked away, keen to distance herself from him.

"And now for a special announcement," Jocelyn continued, "I mentioned earlier how fortunate we were to have prolific best-selling author Mr Edward De'Ath with us. He has kindly agreed to mentor a writer for the duration of the week here. He's willing to allow someone to shadow him, and act as their mentor. He's very generously agreed to assess their work and assist in any way he can in tightening up their manuscript. It's a fantastic opportunity for someone, I'm sure you'll all agree."

More applause filled the room.

Ruby's tummy clenched. A feeling of dread ran through her. God no . . . please no. Her heart started pounding. That couldn't be the prize, surely? Dead-Ed being her mentor – it'd be the biggest booby prize ever. An inner voice urged her to get away so she didn't have to continue the farce. She eyed-up the exits which were fire doors so she couldn't go out of those. It would have to be the entrance where they'd come in. She turned round – the doors were closed. There was only one option as far as she could see. Fake feeling sick and make a run for it. Who'd care? They'd barely notice her departure. She could wait outside for Verity, apologise and explain she was feeling the heat and needed some fresh air.

Jocelyn continued. "The committee tried to think of a fair way to give everyone a chance to benefit from the marvellous opportunity . . ."

Ruby reached forward for her handbag, but the woman on the row in front must have moved her chair because her handbag strap was caught under the leg.

Bugger.

"So," Jocelyn carried on, "before you all arrived, we taped an envelope to the underside of each chair."

Delegates began to shuffle.

"Every single envelope has a piece of paper inside . . . only one has *winner* written on it. We shuffled the pack numerous times and asked the staff to tape the envelopes to the chairs. Right now, we have no idea who has the winning seat, therefore, without further ado, do you want to all check your envelopes and call out if you have the winning ticket. This should be quite fun."

Fun? Was she having a laugh?

While delegates scrambled for the envelopes attached to the bottom of their chairs, Ruby sat as rigid as a statue, as if by doing so, she couldn't possibly win. Verity quickly retrieved her envelope and whipped it open, "Nope, not me. That's a shame," she nudged Ruby's arm, "from what I've seen online, he looks quite hot."

"Anybody yet?" Jocelyn's voice screeched over the noise of everyone opening their envelopes.

"Why aren't you checking yours?" Verity asked.

Ruby screwed up her face, "I don't tend to win stuff."

"Have a look, you never know," Verity's fixed stare gave her no choice but to bend down to retrieve her envelope. If she didn't, it would look odd. Particularly as the two ladies sitting next to Verity that she'd shoved along, were clutching blank tickets and both were looking expectantly at her also.

Please no, not me Ruby silently willed, bracing herself that any minute she was going to have to deliver a performance worthy of an Oscar. There was little doubt in her mind the winning ticket would have her name on it.

Jocelyn's voice came over the mic again. "Someone must have it by now. Do call out if you've got the ticket."

Ruby tore at the edge of her envelope and reached inside to pull out the small piece of paper. As she unfolded it, the word *winner* flashed before her eyes, taunting her, the grim reality of what the ticket meant sinking in. She could have cried.

"Oh my God," Ruby's hand theoretically flew to her mouth, "I can't believe it."

Verity raised her hand, "Over here."

Jocelyn's voice came through the mic, "I do believe we have our winner on the back row. Could you stand up with your ticket so everyone can see?"

Ruby forced her best *I've won* smile as she stood and held the ticket in the air. Jocelyn leaned into the mic. "What's your name, please?"

"Ruby," she called to the packed hall.

"Well done, Ruby, you're going to have a fabulous week. Let's all give Ruby a round of applause, shall we." Jocelyn proceeded to give rapturous applause with everyone joining in.

Ruby's fixed grin made her jaw ache. Inside she was grimacing. Mentoring from Dead-Ed – she'd rather stick pins in her eyes. What the bloody hell was Neil thinking of? And who the hell did he know at the writing school to have facilitated it?

No way was she having anything to do with the stupid fiasco.

No way at all.

9.

Ed had entered the hall a few minutes later than the others. Garth had been at the front near the stage with the other committee members, but he didn't want to move past everyone so he'd seated himself in a corner at the back of the hall. Seemingly the welcome meeting was only about fifteen minutes and then drinks before dinner.

He'd listened to Jocelyn's welcome which was fine, but the rest of the crap involving him mentoring was a huge surprise and absolutely not going to happen. Of all the women in the hall, the infuriating Ruby redhead had won the prize. When Garth had previously asked him if he'd be up for *doing a bit of mentoring,* he'd implied it was more of an hour's session reading a couple of chapters of a novel, not spending the whole week with someone. And, as his friend had only mentioned it the once, and said nothing more, he'd completely forgotten about it. The task now was to find Garth, ASAP. Not a smidgeon of a chance would he be spending any time with demon car crash Red . . . how could a relaxing few days turn out to be a such a nightmare? He had to put a stop to it. As he tried to move along out of the hall, others weren't in a rush so he shuffled along behind them, willing them forward. Boy, did he need a drink.

A short woman in front of him was speaking to the lady next to her. "You were unlucky sitting so close to the woman that won the prize, pity you didn't get that winning seat."

"I know," the younger of the two replied, "and it could have been my seat. I was going to move into it when the chap sitting there left, but the red-haired woman slotted in as quick as a flash and almost begged me to hitch up to let her friend sit next to her. She even made her friend sit on the inside seat so she could have the aisle one. I reckon something was going on there. I'm telling you, it has fix written all over it if you ask me."

"What, like she knew that seat had the winning ticket? They said it was random."

"I know, but she said something about she couldn't sit in the inside as she got cramp so wanted to be on the aisle seat. I hitched along as it seemed mean not to. And wham bam, she suddenly wins the prize. What's all that about?"

"That's so unfair. It smells a bit fishy . . . as if she knew that was the winning seat."

"Yeah, makes you wonder. Never mind, I reckon it's better mingling with everyone here as opposed to being stuck with a mentor all week, good looking as he might be," she sniggered, clearly having no idea he was right behind them. Ed quickly veered left and slipped past them so they wouldn't notice him.

The woman must be wrong, surely? It couldn't possibly have been a fix. No way. Ruby redhead would

62

be no more interested in spending any time with him than he would with her. She'd smashed into the back of his car, for God's sake. Normally he was fairly calm and laid back, but right now, he could throttle Garth for not clarifying this mentoring crap. Well, he could just go and do one. There wasn't a cat in hell's chance he was spending any time with the fiery Red. They'd have to get someone else.

Outside of the hall, he brusquely made his way past the seated lawn area, through the conservatory and back to the bar. Right now, beer wasn't going to cut it. Something much stronger was in order. Imagine spending any time with that madam. It'd be a car crash, literally. While he waited to be served, he gazed around at the mixture of delegates wearing yellow lanyards, and white badgers eagerly trying to engage by joining in with the laughter and chatting. Thankfully, Ruby redhead with her winning ticket, was nowhere to be seen. But neither was Garth.

Where the hell was he?

Hiding no doubt – knowing he was in for it, big time.

"What can I get you, sir?" the barman cut into his thoughts.

Ed blew out a breath. "Whisky. And make it a double!"

10.

"You know damn well I didn't sign up for this mentoring crap." Ed took a swig of his whisky, "And how come out of every single person that possibly could have won the chance to shadow me, I get the hot bloody redhead."

"Ohhhh, think she's hot, do we?"

Ed huffed. "I meant fiery. She pranged my car for God's sake."

Gareth had the grace to look remorseful, "It does seem a bit awkward, I must say."

"Awkward! It's a bleeding disaster. How many delegates did you say are here?" Ed didn't wait for an answer, "over two hundred you said. So, what the hell was the chance of getting her?"

"Pretty remote I would have thought. But if it's any consolation, her face was a picture when she had to stand up and everyone clapped. I don't think she's overjoyed either."

"No, I bet. You need to think of a way to get me out of it!"

"How?" Garth scowled, "there's not much I can do. You'll have to just grin and bear it, mate."

"I don't think so. Have you access to her booking details?"

"No. Why?"

"I'd like to know more about her."

"What for? She's only shadowing you for a few days, you're not about to marry the woman. Anyway, shush, Jocelyn's with her and it looks like she's bringing her over."

"In that case," Ed emptied his glass, "I'll be going for an early night. I am not sitting and socialising with her. Nor Jocelyn either."

Garth grabbed his arm as he attempted to move off the sofa, "For God's sake, you can't go yet. They're here now."

Jocelyn, Red and a third woman approached them. Jocelyn gave a big, *it's going well so far* smile. "Hello again, I thought it would be nice for our mentorship winner to meet you, Edward."

"Actually I prefer Ed."

"Oh, right, Ed it is then. Ruby, if you don't already know, this is Ed De'Ath who you'll be spending time with, and this is Garth who's on the committee. They're friends from their uni days."

Ed noticed Ruby gritting her teeth. "Pleased to meet you," she said, looking anything but. Totally ignoring him, she spoke directly to Garth, "This is Verity, she and I just met today for the first time."

"Please," Garth gestured to the spare seats, "why don't you join us, we've got about twenty minutes before dinner?"

"Before we get comfy," Jocelyn smiled at Ed, "could I get a photo of you, Ruby and I? I thought we could do a blog about the week for you both. We'll get another photo on the last day to see how it's worked out. It might be good to put it in the newsletter, what do you think, Garth?"

"Yeah, great idea."

Bloody traitor

"Can you take it, Garth?" Jocelyn turned to him, "Ed, maybe you in the middle of Ruby and I. I think that'd be better."

Redhead's sour face was a picture. Ed couldn't see a way out that wouldn't appear childish, so found himself shanghaied into posing for the photo between the two of them. Jocelyn wasn't a problem, but being forced to get closer to Ruby was. A whiff of her musky perfume aroused his senses more than it should have done. Did she have any idea how sensual and seductive the aroma was? Course she did. With a face and figure like she had, she'd be well aware of her attraction and know how to use it.

"Come on, guys," Garth encouraged. "Say cheese!"

Forcing a smile, Ed moved away as soon as was appropriate while Jocelyn took her phone back and put it away in her bag. She smiled at Ruby and Verity, "I'll leave you with Garth, he's an ambassador this evening so will be hosting a white badgers table tonight. Maybe the girls can join your table, Garth?"

"Absolutely."

"Good. I'll catch up with you later then. Have fun all of you."

Fun? Whatever table Garth was hosting, Ed was going to be on a different one. He wasn't eating dinner with Ruby Red. No way.

The women took their seats on the sofa, Ruby the furthest away from him, thank God. She began to speak in a charming kind of way, as if trying to demonstrate she could be nice. And her voice was rather soft and sultry when she was being pleasant and not arguing, "I think it's a great idea that they have allocated tables for anyone here for the first time, don't you, Verity?"

"Yes, it's a nice touch."

"It does work well," Garth agreed, "the last thing we want is anyone feeling alone on the first evening. And tomorrow, you're able to dine wherever; tonight's just a bit of an ice-breaker."

"Are you dining with us, Ed?" Verity asked.

"Course he is," Garth chipped in, abruptly stopping any chance he had to make up an excuse, "he's hosting with me tonight."

Heat was creeping up his neck. It'd look pretty juvenile if he objected now. He stifled a sigh of frustration. If he was going to have to tolerate her for one night, then so be it – he certainly wasn't going to another, he'd make that abundantly clear to Garth.

He barely joined in with the before dinner pleasantries. They soon got onto the subject of their own writing accomplishments, it sounded like Red hasn't got that far. With a bit of luck she might not have a complete manuscript. Or was that wishful thinking? Apart from occasionally nodding and answering any questions directed at him, he remained silent. It wasn't the best pre-dinner behaviour, he knew that, but he didn't want to make small talk, not with her anyway. However, as twitchy as he was, he couldn't help his eyes straying more closely to her. She was stunning; there was no doubt about that. His preference was for tall women, and her long legs enhanced by her tight denim jeans put her at a nice height for him. She was wearing strappy sandals and normally feet wouldn't interest him that much, he was more attuned to the obvious feminine attributes. But his eyes betrayed him and became fixated on her delicate toes, highlighted with subtle pink nail varnish. The decorative gold sandals enhanced her elegant feet, and the pretty, silver ankle chain peeping out from the bottom of her jeans was incredibly sexy. He felt the blood drain from his face, and he knew exactly where it was going instead. While he told himself that he didn't like her at all, he couldn't fail to appreciate she was a beautiful young woman.

He made his excuses for a bathroom break.

She was getting under his skin in more ways than one.

11.

Hearing the buzzer from the dining room indicating dinner was being served, Ed returned after a breather outside and waited in the queue at the server. After selecting lasagne, salad and garlic bread, he made his way towards the adjacent eating area to the table Garth was sitting at. Red was already seated at the circular table with a couple of others he hadn't yet been introduced to. She raised her hand and he thought initially that his eyes were deceiving him and she was waving him over. She must have thought that too as she quickly called out, "Over here, Verity." Her friend approached the table the same time as he did. "We've just made it, Ed," Verity smiled at him as she pulled out her chair, "It looks like we're a full house now."

Ed breathed a sigh of relief, taking his seat opposite Red. The last thing he wanted was to be next to her and having to make conversation.

"I know we've all got our badges on," Garth said, "but shall we go round the table and introduce ourselves. I'm Garth, on the committee. I've been coming for the last four years. He turned to the two ladies to his left. A small plump lady, probably the oldest of them all, Norma greeted them, and the second lady, mid-forties, gave her name as Wendy. There were two blokes, Myles looked to be early forties with a huge birthmark on the right side of his face, and Paul with a bald head, was maybe sixtyish. Red was the youngest of them all, and her mate, Verity, probably a good eight to ten years older, introduced herself. She was attractive enough with salon styled dark hair and beautiful brown eyes, but couldn't hold a candle to the allure of Red.

It was his turn. "I'm Ed, guest lecturer."

"And prolific author," Norma gushed, "you must be such a busy man. I've read all of your books and loved each of them."

"Then I'm delighted to be sitting with you, Norma. Thank you."

He noticed that Red was moving food around her plate but not appearing to put any in her mouth when Wendy spoke to her, "You are lucky Ruby to have the winning ticket for Ed to mentor you. I bet you're so excited about the week." Before she had chance to reply, Verity, her cheeks flushed from the pre-dinner wine, turned to the others around the table, "It was nearly me," she giggled, "but Ruby made me change seats."

Ruby's face coloured with embarrassment, "I'm not sure it was exactly like that, Verity. I only asked for the end seat as my legs are quite long. I do it all the time, you know, like on an aircraft."

Me thinks she is protesting too much. Something didn't add up about her, especially as she abruptly changed the subject and asked, "Are any of you published yet, apart from Ed, of course?" The conversation continued around the table centring on what level everyone appeared to be at with their writing. Garth excelled at *holding court*, while Ed continued to eat and surreptitiously observe Ruby. He'd never been a lover of red-haired women, but he had to admit, hers was stunning. The thickness of it cascaded around her face in huge waves. The colour was most unusual – it was vibrant and appeared completely natural. Put that with her striking turquoise green eyes, it all added up to a desirable femme fatale. But redheads were dangerous. His mother was one and she'd abandoned him and his brother when she'd got a better offer. His dad had been forced to take on all the domestic chores as well as trying to earn a living. It can't have been easy parenting two boisterous children on his own. Ed had been a good child, studious and trying to help, his brother not so. He'd always been trouble and continued to be into adulthood – in fact he was still trouble with a capital T.

As Ed reached for the water jug, his antenna sprang up when Myles asked Red what she did for a living.

"Admin. What about you?" she asked rather quickly.

***

Ruby picked at her food and eventually put her knife and fork together. She remained seated and didn't go to the server for a dessert as the others did. The lies were difficult to keep up, especially with Dead-Ed's scrutiny. At least she was trying to be pleasant. Thank goodness Norma was hogging him so she could chat to the others. It was noticeable that he could be charming when he wanted to be; he seemed to be a good conversationalist with everyone, that is, everyone except her. Verity had joked in the hall about him being hot, never was a truer word spoken. Not that he appealed to her. But she couldn't deny his attractiveness. That's why Sophie had succumbed to a one-night stand with him after a conference.

"While I've got you all here," Garth said, tucking into his Eton Mess, "I need to know if there are any budding actors amongst us that are up for a bit of drama?"

"What sort of drama?" Verity frowned.

"Don't look so worried, it's just taking part in a play. We have what's affectionately called Stage Shenanigans. Prior to coming here, delegates submit a short play, which is very short, only six minutes to be exact. The plays are judged by an independent company and they select six to be performed on the stage in the hall. This year, my entry has been selected, which means I can finally call myself a script writer," he chuckled. "Now all the playwrights need are delegates to volunteer as actors and to make us shine."

"There wouldn't be long to rehearse though would there?" Myles asked.

"No, not really. But to be honest, there is very little rehearsal required. In fact, the actors invariably have the script in their hand so they can read their lines. It's quite light of heart. And the audience get to judge the winning play and someone gets best actor. It's quite fun."

"It sounds like it," Verity smiled, "I'd be up for it."

"Great I'll put you down. On Monday afternoon the actors are cast, there's a rehearsal and then again the following afternoon. The plays are performed on Tuesday evening. Any takers?" Garth asked looking expectantly at them all.

"Not for me," Paul smiled, "but I'll enjoy watching them."

"Me too," Norma said, "I'm no good at acting."

Garth turned to Ed, "What about you mate, can I tempt you to take part?"

"I don't think so. I'm not sure acting's my thing to be honest."

"You might be surprised."

Dead-Ed put his knife and fork together. "What's your play about, exactly?"

"It's about a married woman who's just given birth. Her husband believes the wife has been having an affair and the baby isn't his."

"And has she been having an affair?"

"Ah, well that's for the audience to judge, but let's just say there's a humorous twist." Garth playfully tapped his nose, "I can't say any more at this stage."

"It sounds like a lot of fun," Verity said, "How many actors do you need?"

"Three. A husband, a wife, and a sister. But for now, my lips are sealed. It's just light hearted, I don't see it winning or anything, there are some really talented script writers here. But I have enjoyed doing it."

"That's the main thing then," Wendy said, "I try and tell my grandchildren it's the taking part that counts, but they look at me as if I've grown an extra head." She rolled her eyes, "What about you, Ruby? Are you going to have a go at acting?"

"It sounds great but it's not for me," she put on an apologetic face, "sorry. I'm sure there'll be plenty that want to take part, though." She poured herself a glass of water.

Nobody would have any idea she was becoming quite an accomplished actor already.

12.

It was relatively cool at 5.45 a.m. as Ed began his early morning run around the lake adjacent to the accommodation. There was plenty of light breaking through the trees, perfect conditions for exercise. And he'd wanted to be early. Seemingly there was morning meditation by the lake and the last thing he wanted was to be caught up with a bunch of women chanting on yoga mats.

It wasn't going to be a long run, but a pleasant short one he thought. He set off, more of a jog initially. He always found early morning the best part of the day. Before starting any writing, he had to go out for a run. He used it as thinking and plotting time. Although he had an indoor gym at home, he preferred exercising outdoors. He'd done so much running initially when Laura had died. Almost to exhaustion. As if it might somehow make the pain go away. But it never did.

As he was coming to the end of his run, out of the corner of his eye, he spotted another early starter about to begin a run around the lake. And it didn't take him more than a second to realise who it was. Red was in Lycra shorts that clung to her tight backside and a vest top hugging her pert breasts. The black colour made her skin lighter. She'd tied her hair up in a ponytail on the top of her head which made her look cute. As she was about to set off jogging, she must have heard someone behind her. He watched her turn as the chap that had stood on the stage the previous evening and introduced himself as the manager, approached her. Whatever he was saying, she looked uncomfortable. He barely knew the girl, but sensed her tension. He was too far away to ascertain what was being said, but he knew by her body language, she wasn't comfortable. Why was the manager out at this time in the morning and loitering around the lake – shouldn't he be folding napkins or something?

Ed purposely made his way away from the main path so she wouldn't see him. He took a seat on a bench rather than meeting up with her – that was the last thing he wanted. Not that she'd stop and chat, her dislike of him was evident. But he didn't want to pass her and have to acknowledge her with a good morning greeting. He still needed to see Garth and somehow renege on this mentorship nonsense. It'd be best for them both as he was certain she wouldn't want to do it anymore than he did. He'd be doing them both a favour by backing out.

When she came past, she wouldn't see him as the bench was obscured by fern trees. And he'd noticed she was wearing earbuds so no doubt the music would drown any noise out. Nevertheless, when his phone vibrated in his shorts pocket and he saw the caller was his PA in New York, he moved further back, away from the main path.

"Hi Carolyn, how's it going?" he glanced at his watch, "what are you doing up at this time?"

"The usual insomnia so I thought I'd try you before you started lecturing. Can you speak?"

"Yeah, sure, is everything okay?"

"All good, honey," she drawled in her New York accent. "I'm sorry to bother you, but I thought I'd better let you know, Michael's called."

Michael, his errant brother getting in touch could only mean one thing . . . trouble.

"What's up with him now?"

"The usual. And he's whining because you aren't answering his calls. He wants to know if you're still in London or back in the US."

"Has he said what he wants, as if I don't already know?"

"Yeah, the usual, I'm afraid. Says he's likely to be evicted so needs to speak to you."

Ed sighed. Money was a regular request from Michael. He was intending to reply to his calls, but he'd been putting it off. They didn't spend time together like normal brothers, it was more about him lecturing him on his lifestyle. Michael drifted from job to job, and woman to woman. He regularly hooked up with women attracted initially to him with his cheeky-chappy personality, but it always ended once they saw the real Michael De'Ath. And by then, he'd usually squandered any money he'd had, and was back for more.

"Transfer him four thousand dollars. That'll tide him over until I speak to him."

"Okay." He could hear disappointment in Carolyn's voice but she knew better than to question him. And even though she must have been fed up with Michael's constant phone calls when he couldn't get in touch with Ed, she, nor many people knew the reason why he was his Achilles' heel. He never shared with anyone the promise he'd made to his late father. Even on his death bed, all his father's thoughts had been about. Michael. 'Look after him, Ed, always. He's not strong like you. You need to be his father now. Promise me you will take care of him.' And Ed had done exactly that even though the errant Michael would try the patience of Mother Theresa.

"What about when he calls again," Carolyn asked, "he says he needs to speak to you."

"I'll contact him when I leave here."

"He sounded cross that you're not answering."

"Yeah, I bet."

"Says he's tried several times."

"Yes, he has. But I'm busy right now and don't need to be distracted by his woes."

"That's what I said . . . well, not quite like that, just that you were lecturing."

"Fine. I'll ring him later. He won't bother you once you've transferred the money. That's all he's interested in, not me. Anyway, while I've got you, Carolyn, can you do something for me?"

"Yes, what is it?"

"I need you to find out what you can about a female, mid-twenties, called Ruby Lowe. Maybe speak to Alison, she might be able to help." Alison was part of the agency that facilitated any of his book signing tours in the UK.

"Okay. Have you an address?"

"No, I'm afraid not. But it's in London." He'd heard her telling Myles the previous evening she lived and worked in London.

"Right. Anything else that might help?" she asked, in a *you aren't giving me much to go on* voice.

"She's registered here at the writer's school. I've got the details of the car hire company she's rented her Toyota from. Have you got a pen handy?" He relayed the information he had.

"Okay, I'll see what I can find out. It's a bit of a tall order."

"Yeah, I know. Do your best. And I need to know sooner, rather than later."

After a few more details about work, he cut the call. Red could be perfectly innocent, but he doubted it. There was some sort of agenda going on with her and he was determined to find out what. The winning chair bothered him. Something didn't add up. His eyes roamed around the lake. Red was nowhere to be seen so he jogged back to Lakeside Plus. She was best avoided. Dinner the previous evening was more than enough. And, as if that wasn't bad enough, he'd tossed and turned until the early hours wrestling in his mind why he couldn't stop thinking about her and came up with the conclusion it was because he'd got landed with the mentoring malarkey. What else could it be? She was feisty . . . far too feisty for him, so it was nothing like that. No, it was more that he had to get rid of the irritating woman. Just because she had a figure to rival a catwalk model, legs like a gazelle and hair that any man would like to run his fingers through – he wasn't remotely attracted to her. That said, as he stepped into the shower, he couldn't get the image of her out of his mind . . . how hot she looked in tight running gear clinging to every sinew of her body.

He reached for the shower thermostat and turned it to cold.

13.

After a dreadful night's sleep tossing and turning, Ruby had been awake at the crack of dawn and decided to head for a run around the lake. It was early, but light so nothing to worry about in terms of safety. It was a writer's retreat after all. Had she known Daryl was going to accost her, she'd never have bothered at all. He made her jump as she didn't hear him approach her. He was wearing a shirt and trousers so clearly not there for exercise.

"Good morning," he said, "what a beautiful day it's going to be. You're going for a run I take it?" His leering eyes blatantly ran up and down her body.

"Yes, I want to crack on so I can get back and showered before the lectures start."

"Well, don't skip breakfast whatever you do, the kitchen do a great fry up."

"I'll check that out, thank you. Right, I'd better make a start."

"Before you do, I thought we could have a drink together tonight?"

"I don't think so," she said, rather quickly. He scowled. The Daryls of this world didn't like rejection.

"Why?"

"Because I'll be busy. There's a lot going on that I want to get involved in."

"Yeah, but you can fit a quick drink in, surely?"

"Look, I'm not being funny, but I'm not here to be having drinks with random men I don't know."

"But you do know me," he said, "I'm the man that got you what you came here for. And I don't suppose you want that little nugget to get out?" He raised an eyebrow. "And remember, I know you're not here to *get involved with activities* – you're here for a purpose and as I've already helped you, I reckon you owe me a drink at least."

It was pointless arguing with him. She'd come across his type so many times. It was clear he wasn't going to take no for an answer. "Okay, but maybe not tonight. I'll look at the programme and see what I'm doing. I'll catch you later, yeah?"

"Brilliant, I'll look forward to it. I'll be around. See ya."

She set off gently jogging, keen to get away from him. How did he know she'd be by the lake at that time in the morning? He must have been watching for her coming out of the accommodation block. Was he looking at CCTV and waiting for her to leave her room? She increased her pace. Even though he'd asked her to have a drink with him, she had no intention of doing so. But him hinting that he might expose her, left her with no option than to agree, just to get rid of him. That encounter between them meant she needed to move faster than she originally thought.

Returning to her room, she showered as best she could with the shower curtain sticking to her legs regardless of how many times she tried to extract it. Daryl had unnerved her. If he was watching her movements, it was creepy. Her tummy plummeted when she thought of a worse scenario. With him being the manager, he'd have access to a master key to the delegates' rooms. She knew his type only too well. He wanted much more than a friendly drink. Sadly for her, it had been an agenda from the opposite sex from an early age. Men were drawn to her looks. It wasn't conceit that she knew she was attractive, it was the attention she'd always had. With red hair and green eyes, men always wanted to screw her. There was a section of women she'd come across in life that didn't like her either. Yet she never used her looks for anything. It wasn't as if she even fancied any of the men that came onto her. She never did. Even those she had relationships with, she didn't enjoy the physical side of things. Now, because of Daryl, her task was to get the specimen from Dead-Ed for DNA testing, sooner rather than later. Neil had thought he was helping no doubt, but he wasn't. In her experience, men like Daryl Hill always wanted payment for services rendered. And how did Neil know him, even?

Ruby made herself a coffee and sat at the small desk, waiting until she heard the housekeepers milling about on the corridor. She'd previously heard Dead-Ed's door bang and assumed he'd headed off for breakfast. The programme indicated breakfast was eight until nine with lessons beginning at nine-thirty. As she sipped her coffee, her whole focus was how she could retrieve something personal of his. There wasn't a plan B, she had to come away with something and the best option was his toothbrush. Her ears were tuned in to the corridor. When she heard the housekeepers coming closer, she tentatively left her room to approach his. The smaller of two women opened his door. "A bit of a come-down from New York, I reckon," she said to her buddy.

Ruby hovered in the doorway until the ladies noticed her. "Good morning," she greeted them brightly. "This is rather awkward," she cleared her throat, "I think I left my contact lenses in . . . er . . . in Mr De'Ath's bathroom," she faked embarrassment, "last night. Would you mind if I popped in for a second to take a look?"

"Contact lenses?" the housekeeper raised her eyebrows and judging by her expression, the penny had dropped that she must have been intimate with Dead-Ed. Ruby didn't care. It was a means to an end. "Hang on a second, I'll take a look for you."

"It's okay," Ruby tried to move forward, "I can check myself."

"No. Please if you don't mind," the woman pulled a pained face, "it's more than my job's worth to let you into Mr De'Ath's room, we've been told to be careful. He gets women following him about, trying to snoop on him," she raised her eyebrows, "because he's a famous author and all that."

"Ah, I see," Ruby nodded, furious her plan had been thwarted.

"Not that you're one of them," the housekeeper flushed, "I don't think that for a minute."

"Oh, good," Ruby gave a fake laugh, "I wouldn't want you to think that."

"Just give me a second and I'll have a look." The housekeeper went into the bathroom. She wouldn't have much to look at – the bathrooms were tiny.

"Nope, I can't see anything here on the shelf," she came back to the doorway, "are you sure you left them in the bathroom?" The housekeeper's gaze swept around the room towards the desk. "I can't see anything in here, either." From where Ruby was standing in the doorway, she couldn't see a thing out of place. The room looked barely used.

Ruby shook her head. "Not entirely sure, no. Not to worry, I'll have another look in my room. Thank you anyway." Turning on her heel, she hastily took off, praying the housekeeper wouldn't say anything to Dead-Ed. How could she possibly explain that pack of lies? But then again, the staff had to be discreet. They might have a laugh amongst themselves, but they'd hardly be approaching any delegates about sleeping arrangements. No, that was most unlikely.

She blew out a breath as she closed her room door. If she could have just nicked his toothbrush, she'd have been out of there and heading down the M1 to London. Now, she was going to have to be in the insufferable man's company for at least another day until she came up with something else. And there was also creepy Daryl to contend with.

Damn, damn, damn.

14.

Ed left the dining room straight after a hearty egg and bacon breakfast to make his way to the hall for his first teaching session. His whole life was about being prepared – hence the need to make sure the IT was all set up. If it failed, he was well able to fill the hour, but he liked organisation. For those with a visual learning style, he had slides, and he'd be setting short writing tasks for the delegates to break up the monotony of him talking. Most writers, whether novice or experienced, liked to share their work so he always allowed time for feedback in a session of any writing tasks he'd set. He'd encourage those that were hesitant to read what they'd come up with. Although he could sense their nerves, he knew they would benefit from doing so. The times he'd done sessions over the years and spoken to delegates that had read out their work, invariably they'd expressed their thanks. Like another step on the writing journey. And as he always said at the end of his sessions when he concluded on the learning, writing a book and publishing one is only the beginning. The next challenge was marketing. And every author has to do that which maybe could be something as simple as reading a passage at a book club, to moving on to public speaking. So, it was good to start early and *dip a toe in the water.*

As he scrolled through his PowerPoint presentation, the tech bloke called to him from a booth at the side of the hall, "Can you grab the lapel mic and we'll test the sound?"

Ed switched it on and said a few words, got the nod all was working and left it on the table so he could step outside the hall to welcome those arriving for the session. In his opinion, teaching went better if the delegates felt an affinity to the presenter, therefore greeting them as they arrived, he liked to do where possible. In the US, he wasn't able due to the size of the audiences that came to see him. But they were lecturing sessions opposed to teaching.

"Morning, mate," Garth sauntered into the empty hall and made his way to the small stage. "All set?" he asked.

"Yeah, all ready. I'm just going to nip outside so I'm there for everyone arriving."

"Why's that?"

"It works well. An audience responds better if they've met you beforehand."

"Well, you learn something new every day. I didn't know that."

"It's not always possible, but here it's ideal. Oh, I've been thinking. Can you get me out of this mentoring malarkey? I really don't want Ruby with me for the rest of the week."

"I thought you'd settled down about that?"

"No, I haven't."

"I don't know why," Garth scowled, "she's lovely."

"To you she might be, but not to me."

"But you did say you'd do some mentoring."

"Yeah, reading chapters of a novel. And I'd imagined I'd get someone . . . normal . . . not sex on legs."

"Ah, I see. Still denying you've got the hots for her, then?"

"I've told you, I bloody well don't have the *hots* for her," Ed snapped, "far from it."

"Alright, alright, calm down."

"I'm not interested, so get that right out of your head. Can you speak to one of the other lecturers and see if they're willing to mentor her?"

"I could ask I suppose," Garth shrugged, "not sure what I can say though as an excuse for you not doing it."

Ed sighed. "Maybe something along the lines of I'm not feeling one hundred percent."

"Okay, I can give it a try."

He slapped Garth's back, "You do that, buddy."

Ed leant on the metal handrail outside the hall, greeting delegates as they arrived.

"Good morning, Ed," Norma, the sweet older lady who'd sat beside him at dinner the previous evening smiled as she approached. Paul, a fellow dinner companion was walking beside her.

"Morning both of you, thanks for coming."

"I wouldn't have missed it," Paul said, "I'm hoping it's going to improve my work in progress."

"Let's hope it does then."

"The girls are coming, they'll be along in a minute," Norma said, "they're just powdering their noses."

He gave a false grin, "Brilliant. See you in a minute."

He'd wondered if Red would come. In fairness to her, she probably felt she ought to with this mentoring debacle. Thankfully that'd be sorted shortly so she'd be one less thing on his mind. He could avoid her then. Garth was spot on implying he found her hot. She was hot. You'd have to be a blind man not to see that. Everything about her screamed of sensuality. But it didn't mean he wanted to get her into bed. Since Laura died, he hadn't been immune to attractive women. Most liaisons had been more than satisfactory, even though half the time he felt they were more interested in sleeping with his status, rather than the man.

As the final delegates strolled up, Verity and Red were amongst them. Could Red get any more attractive? Gone was the sexy goddess running attire and in its place was a delicately pretty, lemon dress and white plimsolls. The dress was short, cut above the knee, showing off her long, toned legs, beautifully. And that hair, cascading around her shoulders, added an extra feminine touch. He knew from writing, long hair in a woman appealed to the male of the species because it was associated with health, youth and reproductive vigour.

"Good morning," he greeted them both, barely able to look at Red. He daren't. Because all he could visualise was her thick mane of red hair spread across his pillow.

15.

Ruby sat with Verity well away from the front. She knew that in adult education a lecturer wouldn't pick on anyone to answer questions, but after the mentorship fiasco the previous evening, she wanted to blend in well away from Dead-Ed. And Verity was fairly amiable so wasn't bothered where they sat. She had no choice really but to come to his session, it would look odd if she hadn't with this so-called mentoring claptrap. And, she had to keep reminding herself, she was actually there to try and get close enough to him to get something personal for testing. What that would be now she hadn't got his toothbrush, she hadn't yet thought. But she wouldn't be able to do anything stuck in another classroom.

"Hey," Verity said, reaching in her bag for her notebook and pen, "that manager bloke . . . Daryl, he's interested in you, you know. I could tell the way he came over to us in the dining room. All that rubbish about where we enjoying our breakfast, I reckon it was just a way to talk to you."

Ruby pulled a face, "I'm hoping he's just being friendly 'cause I'd seen him by the lake first thing when I went for a run."

"Oh, right. Was he running, then?"

"No, I think he was on his way to the main building or something. We only said hello."

"So, he'd already seen you by the lake, and then comes into the dining room to see you again. I'm telling you, he's after you."

"God, I hope not."

"Have you got a boyfriend?"

"No. I did have but we split up recently." Ruby's tummy still felt tense remembering how Daryl had slyly approached her in the dining room when she'd only seen him less than an hour earlier. She took her iPad out of her bag and switched it on. "You're lucky being married; you don't have this sort of hassle."

"No, I suppose so, but that doesn't mean I don't appreciate an attractive man." Verity rested her notebook and pen on her knee, "Take Ed for instance, he's pretty hot don't you think?"

Ruby frowned indifference, "To you maybe, not to me."

"Shame. I was reading about him last night, he lost his wife a couple of years ago."

"Really? I didn't know that." She genuinely didn't.

"Yeah, it's sad. But that means he's single if you did like him."

"No, honestly, I've had a bellyful of blokes right now. And I'm not really attracted to his type anyway."

She was lying – big time. Ed looked pretty damn hot in a white polo shirt tucked into navy-coloured chino trousers. His brown belt matched his slip-on soft shoes. He was like one of those models in a department store window enticing you to buy the latest male offerings. Not that he was model material though – he was too rugged and masculine for that. She didn't want to notice the way his hair curled at his neck, but her eyes were drawn to it. Even though she didn't like the man, her tummy wasn't tense around him – far from it.

"Good morning," Ed began to speak. While the audience muttered a greeting back, he stepped down from the small stage area so he was level with them. It seemed more intimate somehow. He'd probably done hundreds of presentations so would know how to work an audience.

He cleared his throat. "I'm not going to start today's session with anything about me, only to say I'm author Edward J De'Ath. I write crime fiction and before becoming a novelist, I used to lecture and teach English and creative writing. I'm doing an evening presentation about my writing life, so I won't bore you to death twice. I just want to reiterate what my sessions are going to be about so if you are in the wrong place, you're able to make a hasty retreat, now."

As the delegates sniggered, he nodded to the IT support and a slide filled the screen behind him. The heading was Storytelling. And underneath that was, A beginning, A middle, An End – which brought more mutterings.

"And that's how you write a book," his eyes widened. "Easy peasy. Well, that's what everyone thinks. If only it were that simple, eh? How many times have people said to you, 'I think I'll write a book' – 'I've had such a varied life, I could write a book about it', or 'I've got a great idea for one'. It's as if we rustle them up in our spare time. You're nodding so you clearly agree. People's perception of writing is nothing like reality." He walked backwards towards the small stage and stepped up.

"Before we start, I want to do an exercise with you. Can you for a minute think of a brilliant book you've read – you know what I mean – one that has stayed with you as being an incredible read. You may have recommended it to others." He paused giving them some time to think of one.

"Now, can you all stand up? With that book in mind, please stay on your feet if you can name the publisher. No cheating," he smiled, "I might test you. If you can't remember, it doesn't matter. But sit back down if that's the case."

Ruby's most recent book *Absolutely Perfect* by Justin Credible, she'd bought in Tesco but she had no idea of the publisher so sat down with most of the others. A handful remained standing.

Ed counted them. "So ten of you, out of a class of approximately fifty, know the publishing house of your most recent, cracking book. Okay," he nodded to the few still standing, "take a seat."

He paused for a few seconds.

"The purpose of that exercise is to try and demonstrate that the reader, who ultimately we have to appeal to if we want to sell books, is our biggest champion. They don't really care about the publisher – you can see that by how many of us couldn't remember in this room. So, while I'm fortunate and signed to one of the big five publishing houses, the point I'm trying to demonstrate to you is . . . readers are interested in the story, the written word – very few care about the rest."

Ruby could see many of the audience nodding, clearly appreciating what he was saying which was helpful because many attending the summer school were probably like her, and may have to try independently publishing as a first route. If she ever finished her novel, that is. It was more a leisure accompaniment each evening alongside her being-dumped-wine pick-me-up.

Ed's voice had a melodious quality. It was warm, captivating and engaging. The first task he wanted them to focus on was to take ten minutes to come up with an idea for a novel they'd like to write – either jotting it down or using their iPads. They were to list five bullet points about the novel that they, as the writer wanted in. He suggested they were to consider the genre and setting in the first instance, and emphasised it was purely for the sessions. It didn't have to be anything they would write, it was more an exercise on the best way to do it.

As Ruby watched his delivery, reluctantly she had to admire his charm and charisma. He was a multi-millionaire best-selling author, yet he was giving his time to help at a writers' retreat. Maybe she shouldn't think harshly of him? But then reality kicked in. He had engaged in casual sex and wouldn't face up to his responsibilities – she'd do well to remember that.

During the time he'd given them to write down some points about a proposed novel, she thought back to her task in hand, which had nothing to do with novel writing. As yet, she had zilch on Dead-Ed. Not a single jot. Verity was occupied jotting down what appeared to be a whole first chapter, but still, Ruby tilted her iPad away so if she glanced up, she couldn't see anything. In the search engine, she typed in *specimens that can be used to obtain DNA*. The most common came up repeatedly, buccal swab, which was impossible. A used condom, she shuddered at the thought. There was evidence Dead-Ed was hardly a stalwart for safe sex judging by impregnating her friend, so he more than likely didn't use them, not that she would be sleeping with him to test her theory. She scanned the rest of the list, envelope flaps and postage stamps, not a chance, a cigarette butt – unlikely as he didn't appear to smoke, fingernail clippings, er . . . no. The most obvious were dental floss, a toothbrush, a hairbrush or a razor but there wasn't much chance of that now his room was guarded like a prison. Tissues were a suggested specimen, but again she'd need access to his room and bin, and even then, he may not use tissues.

The final suggestion was a soda can, drinking glass or a straw which were distinct possibilities. The whole place was geared to socialising and the bar; he'd be having plenty to drink while he was there. Yeah, a glass was the best bet. Surely she could slip one he'd drunk out of into her bag – how hard would that be?

16.

"Same time tomorrow," the IT assistant called to Ed as he remained on the stage after everyone had filtered out, gathering his papers and closing his laptop down. Ed was relieved there hadn't been any blips during his first session. IT malfunction irritated the life out of him.

"Yeah, cheers. Sorry, I didn't get your name?"

"Tim."

"Thanks, Tim. I'm here tomorrow and then I believe I get a free day before my two other sessions."

"Yeah, that sounds about right. I'm here with you again in the morning, your session was good by the way."

"Pleased you enjoyed it, and even more pleased you'll be back," he nodded as Tim walked away.

Ed's phone vibrated in his pocket as he placed his laptop in its bag. It was a message from Carolyn, his PA.

Hi Ed, I've done some digging on Ruby Lowe. She's a journalist working for the Northfield Reporter in London. I can't see she has done any actually reporting as there are no articles linked to her name. She's 25 and lives in Fulham. I checked Amazon to see if she's had any novels published. As far as I can see she hasn't, but of course she could publish under a pseudonym. Do you want me to try and find out any more?

He'd got all he needed to know. He messaged back,

That's fine for now.
No need to look for anything else.

In the search engine on his iPhone, he keyed in Northfield Reporter. It was a modest newspaper compared to the mainstream ones, and appeared to concentrate more on celebrities and sensational news as opposed to having any intellectual content.

He made his way out of the hall, with one thing on his mind, which wasn't a reflection on how the morning presentation had gone. Yet again, the exasperating redhead was causing him more unease. What the hell was she really doing there? And why was the newspaper sending a reporter to a writer's retreat? He didn't get it. He was well used to giving interviews that had a monetary remuneration, but what could a newspaper he'd never heard of, be hoping to get out of him? He was hardly likely to be telling his life story to a young journalist without prior agreement. And judging by what he'd already seen, Red didn't look the type to be sucking up to anyone let alone him, for some sort of scoop; he could feel her dislike of him from fifty feet away. He considered the possibility that she was there to get a story on someone else, but quickly dismissed that idea. He was sure the winning ticket fiasco was fixed. She'd known exactly which seat it was on. None of it added up.

In the bright warm sunshine, he made his way towards the lounge, nodded to the delegates sitting at the tables outside, some smoking, most in conversation during the coffee break prior to the next session before lunch.

Garth was coming out of the conservatory towards him as he approached the main building.

"There you are, I was just coming to find you," he motioned to move Ed away to a quiet spot beside a row of laurel bushes. "I've sorted it out. I've spoken to Steve Benford, one of the other lecturers. He's doing *Making Crime Pay* and is willing to step in and mentor Ruby. I told him you weren't feeling brilliant so wasn't sure you could give it your best shot. He's fine about it." He screwed up his face, "I think maybe you ought to tell Ruby though rather than me, it won't be awkward then. She's going to be disappointed, but Steve's a good egg, he'll help her, I'm sure."

"Do you know what," Ed scratched his forehead, "I think I might have been a bit hasty. I ought to do the mentoring really."

Garth scowled, "But you said you didn't want to. What's changed from leaving the classroom to now?" He glanced at his watch, "It's been all of an hour," he said sarcastically.

"Yeah, I know. But it is only for a couple of days, after all."

"I thought you couldn't stand her?"

"I think that's a bit harsh," Ed said. "Maybe I was being judgemental in light of . . . you know, her looks, and she did prang my car."

"Oh, right. So what are you saying now, you're going to be nice to her?"

"Course I am. Why wouldn't I be? Come on, let's grab a coffee."

Garth walked along beside him. "You baffle me sometimes, do you know that."

"Yeah, I baffle myself too," Ed grinned, holding the door for his mate. Gone was the irritation with Red, he was going to be quite the opposite. He could be charming when he wanted to and right now, he really wanted to. He needed to find out exactly what the little madam was up to 'cause he was pretty certain that she wasn't at the summer school to brush up on her writing skills.

17.

With a latte in her hand, Ruby went to find a secluded spot away from the main lounge, mainly to avoid her nemesis. She pulled out a chair, sat down and opened the timetable. As she glanced at the day's lectures, her thoughts were on how she was going to get out of the place – the subterfuge was taking its toll. Her head was still aching since arriving the day before, and she was jumpy, as if her plan was to commit some sort of heinous crime as opposed to getting something personal of Dead-Ed's. Realistically, if she was going to get something, she'd have to put her animosity aside and interact with him, but that was easier said than done. He couldn't be clearer about how he disliked her. She'd noticed how, as he walked around the hall during the writing exercises, he'd nodded and smiled at others, even Verity, yet he'd barely looked at her. And she knew it was deliberate.

Jocelyn, approached her table clutching a mug, "Are you hiding away on your own?"

"No," Ruby shook her head, "not at all. This was the first table I saw free. Verity's just grabbing a coffee. Would you like to join us?"

"Yes, I will do. I'll put my coffee down here and let the boys know where we are. I've just seen them queuing by the coffee machines. Unless you'd like to see if we can get seats in the conservatory?"

"No, I'm fine here. Oh, look, here's Verity now."

"Okay, I'll see what they want to do. I'll be back in a minute."

The boys! She'd hardly label Dead-Ed as a boy. Far from it, he was all man. She chastised herself for noticing – it was a new feeling to her. She liked men, and had cared deeply for Richie, but she couldn't remember her tummy fluttering around him much. Yet, when she first saw Ed that morning, so smart; *he scrubbed up well*, as her gran used to say. And then he'd delivered his session with such confidence and flair, a kaleidoscope of butterflies had descended on her tummy, creating havoc.

"What did you think of Ed's lecture?" Verity asked, putting her cardigan and handbag on the back of the chair. "Wasn't he brilliant?"

"Yeah, very good." Ruby had to rein herself in. He was so much more than very good.

"Are you starting your mentoring with him today?" she asked, sitting down.

"I'm not sure to be honest."

Jocelyn returned with Garth and Ed, clutching coffees and cake. "Here they are. If you're ever looking for them in the future, the cake and biscuit stand's where you'll find them."

They were all chuckling, but not Ed. His eyes were on her, as if he was weighing her up. She felt her cheeks warming and looked away.

102

Jocelyn took a seat next to her and Verity, the *boys* as she referred to them, pulled out the seats opposite. They were in the overflow part of the main building, away from the bar so didn't have the comfy sofas, it was chairs and tables, almost like a dining room.

Jocelyn spoke to Ed as he munched on a piece of lemon drizzle cake. "I'm sorry I missed your session this morning. One of the delegates getting her coffee in front of me was raving about it."

"That's nice." Ed wiped his mouth on a serviette. "What session did you go to?"

"Writing Short Stories. It was good, more me really. I haven't the patience for full length novels. I quite like flash fiction, too."

Jocelyn turned to her and Verity. "How did you girls find Ed's session?"

"It was excellent," Ruby answered with an over-the-top smile.

"I thought so too," Verity joined in. Lots to take in though, I had no idea about some of the stuff you mentioned. I made lots of notes so I don't forget; it was really informative."

Ed grinned, "My head's getting bigger by the minute with all this praise. I'm glad you enjoyed it. There'll be more content in the next session. I don't like to cram too much in on the first one."

"Well, it sounds like you got it just right," Jocelyn almost cooed, "and judging by all this praise, I'm sure you were brilliant."

Did Jocelyn like Ed? She seemed to have more than a friendly agenda the way she was gushing.

"We are so lucky to have got hold of Ed before he returned to New York," Jocelyn went on, "We'd have been really stuck up the proverbial creek without a paddle without him stepping in. How long have you been in London?" she asked Ed, batting her lashes.

"Three weeks. I like to come over once a year to catch up with family."

Yeah, don't we know it, thought Ruby. The last time you were here, you left more than a calling card. And poor Sophie's has to deal with the consequences.

"I might just nip and see if there's any more cake left," Garth said, getting up and moving past Ed, "do you want any if there is?"

"Nah, I'm fine thanks." The others shook their heads.

When he was out of earshot, Verity asked, "What does Garth do for a living, I don't think he's actually said?"

"He's a computer analyst," Ed replied.

"Oh, really, I'd imagined somehow he might teach."

Ed smiled, "I think that was the intention when we went to uni, but when you're that age, you aren't entirely certain what you want to do. He changed direction after a year, while I stayed on the teaching pathway."

"Do you have any regrets about that?" Jocelyn was looking at him all doe-eyed again.

"No, none at all. I always wanted to teach."

Ruby sipped her coffee, dreading the next question would be about what she did for a living.

But Jocelyn carried on, "Shall you be starting the mentoring today?" she turned to her, "I bet you're keen to make a start, Ruby?"

"Oh, yes, dead keen," she said in a voice laced with sarcasm. She couldn't help herself. It was intended for him, but wouldn't be obvious to the others.

Ed's dark eyes honed-in on hers, and if she wasn't mistaken, she saw a teasing glint of mischief in them. "Yes, I thought we might make a start today. How are you fixed right after we've had coffee?" He didn't give her the chance to reply. "I thought we could begin by talking about your current work in progress and how I might be able to help." He raised an eyebrow, "Unless of course there's something on the programme you might want to attend?" That would be the get-out card. If he was expecting her to say no, he was very much mistaken. One way or another, she had to get close to him. She'd already had a missed phone call from Neil, so she really needed to have something to tell him. And she'd be in a much better place getting a receptacle he'd had his mouth around, if she was actually with him.

"Just say if you'd rather not . . . " those eyes again, subtly challenging her? He was expecting her to say no.

"That would be great, thank you," she said, "I'd love to make a start on my own work, even though it's nowhere near complete." She pulled a face.

"That's fine. We can go over the outline of the plot, I think we have an hour before lunch and it is rather lovely outside, if you'd like to sit out there."

"Excuse me." One of the staff interrupted them. "Can I take some of the cups?"

Ruby's eyes were fixated on Ed's mug as the girl piled the used ones in a stack and placed them on a tray. If only she could have grabbed his. She'd be done then and on her way back to London. Of course she couldn't pinch the cup he'd drunk his coffee out of in front of everyone, although she was sorely tempted to grab it and run. She stifled a laugh. How funny would that be? No, she just needed to bide her time and when the opportunity arose, subtly grab something he'd used, and once she had it in the sterile evidence bag hidden in her handbag, she'd be one hundred percent out of there. And it couldn't come a minute too soon. She was still irritated to death being foiled by the housekeepers earlier on – she should have that toothbrush for effort.

"Right," Jocelyn said, "we'd better be making a move to our next sessions. Here's Garth now. Which session are you going to?" she asked him, standing up and tucking her chair in.

Verity grabbed her bag from the back of the chair. "I'll see you at lunch, yeah?"

"Will do," Ruby said, her mouth suddenly dry, even though she'd just had a drink. Everyone leaving made her feel almost bereft. His eyes were on her again, weighing her up. It felt as if she was left behind with the evil monster intent on harming her, while everyone else was going off to have some fun.

"Will you excuse me, please," she said, "I'll just be a minute." She swiftly made her way to the ladies'; she needed some time away to think up some tales to tell him. Tales that'd have nothing to do with a storytelling narrative – more a pack of lies if he asked anything too personal.

18.

As Ruby returned from the lounge, most of the sitting area adjacent to the bar was vacant. Ed had gone from the seats. She made her way through the conservatory and saw him sitting at one of the outside tables. His aviator sunglasses gave him a cool edge. High-end designer ones no doubt.

He was looking pensively across the gardens. The neatly manicured lawns and vast array of mixed border blooms were charming and giving off a pleasant aroma. The whole area with the wooden tables and seating appeared tranquil – it was a perfect venue for writers.

She approached Ed with an uneasy tummy, which was becoming the norm around him. Somehow he made her feel jittery. He was such a good-looking man and wearing sunglasses gave him a sense of style. She delved into her bag for hers, so he wouldn't see her eyes as she made her way towards him. It'd be easier to spin some yarns behind dark shades. Damn that bloody housekeeper. How ridiculous that she wouldn't let her into his room with all the *it's more than our job's worth,* nonsense. She'd been relying on slipping in and out, not expecting for a minute to be foiled. Now she needed to move to a Plan B quickly or she'd end up spending even more days in his company. As she made her way towards him, an idea popped into her head. If she could pull it off, with a bit of luck, she might be able to bring this fiasco to its conclusion quicker than she'd hoped.

"Can I get you some water before I sit down?" she asked. Say yes, she willed knowing she might be able to collect the used plastic cup from him at the end of their session, pretend she was going to bin it, then discretely slip it into her bag instead.

"I'm fine thanks." He reached down to his rucksack and produced a bottle of mineral water. "Maybe get yourself one, though, it is warm out here."

Bugger.

"Okay, I will do." She nipped back indoors to the water dispenser on the corridor, selected two plastic cups and began filling them. Maybe if she placed one for him on the table, he might well take a sip of it. She sighed inwardly. Why was everything so difficult? She took a deep breath in, determined that by the end of the day, she'd have a sample of his DNA, and then she could get out of there.

"I brought you some water in case you ran out," she said, placing the cup on the table in front of him and taking the seat opposite. She felt her phone vibrate in her bag as she placed it on the grass. It'd be Neil – he was best ignored, she had nothing yet to tell him.

"Thanks. You're okay working out here? It's not too hot for you?"

"No, it's fine. I like being hot," she said, then felt herself blushing when realised what she'd said, and now he was grinning. Thank God for the shades.

"I like the heat, too," he said.

She took a glug of the cold water, resisting the temptation to fan her face. "It's lovely out here, so peaceful," she said, glancing around. There were a couple of tables occupied, but most were empty.

"Yeah, most of the delegates are at their next sessions. It'd be even nicer by the lake, but I thought we'd be better making a start here."

Too right. No way did she want to be by the lake with him – that would be way too intimate. All she wanted was for him to drink the water, excuse himself for the loo, then she'd swipe up the cup and skedaddle.

He pushed his sunglasses on top of his head, "I'm glad we've got this opportunity to speak, I think it would be helpful to clear the air." He paused, as if choosing his words carefully, like he'd rehearsed them. "We got off to a bad start and through no fault of either of us, it looks like we've been *thrust* together with this mentoring, and the last thing I want is for you to *feel* uncomfortable."

Thrust together. *Feel* uncomfortable. She'd noticed the emphasis he'd put on the words.

He was grinning again. Or maybe just a normal smile. God, he made her fidgety.

Then another idea came.

"Actually, it's just an idea, but we don't have to do the mentoring, we can sort of pretend. Then you can do your thing, and I'll do mine." Focussing on his dark eyes was a mistake as his scrutiny from under his incredibly long eyelashes made her feel peculiar, almost breathless.

"No mentoring? Are you sure?"

He seemed pleased at that. But she couldn't agree to scrap the mentoring altogether; she needed more time. And she needed to up her game in the pleasantry stakes. But she couldn't be gushing, he'd soon smell a rat.

"Yeah, of course. Although I would really appreciate some help with my novel, so your opinion on the first three chapters would be useful, if you really wouldn't mind. I'd be so grateful for your input." Was that gushing? She wasn't sure. She moved her sunglasses onto her head, "After that, we can call it quits, maybe?"

"Fine by me, but first of all, I'd like to apologise for our little altercation yesterday. I think I was more surprised than anything and that's what caused me to react the way I did. I was rude and it was completely unnecessary. I'm sorry."

Dead-Ed accepting responsibility . . . pity he didn't do that with his child.

"Thanks. I'm sorry, too. I was just worried because it's a hire car."

"So, how about we start again? We have a few days together and I'd like to help you with your writing if you'll let me. After all, you did win that opportunity." He held out his hand . . . "Shall we call a truce?"

"Truce." She let his larger hand wrap around hers, but just as quickly, pulled her hand away as if she'd had an electric shock. Had he felt it too? She took a gulp of her water. Why couldn't he do the same with his – then she'd be gone.

Just take a bloody drink.

He glanced down at his watch. Not your average wristwatch for Mr plenty-of-money. It was a large, silver, gleaming beauty, no doubt a Rolex or similar.

"We have about half an hour before lunch. Why not tell me a bit about yourself? No deep dark secrets," he smiled, "just some background. Where do you live for example?"

Better keep information to a minimum.

"London."

"But you're not originally from London, are you?"

"No, you've guessed."

"Yes, but I'm not quite sure where. You have a well disguised accent."

No way was she telling him anything about herself. Her silence must have spoken volumes as he continued, "What took you to the bright lights of London?"

Sip the water, for God's sake.

"Work."

"I see. What sort of work is that . . . sorry, I don't mean to pry."

Then stop bloody prying.

"It's fine. Admin in an accountants." She was well rehearsed in the lies, but determined to keep them to a minimum. "What about you?" Where are you originally from?"

"Suffolk, but I live in New York now."

Yeah, but you visited London last year, and left an almighty tsunami . . . one you won't even acknowledge.

"How exciting," she said, "I've never been to New York."

"You should visit, it's such a vibrant place, I'm sure you'd fall in love with it."

"I'm sure I would." Spoken like a true millionaire. As if she could ever afford to go to New York. With her debts, she'd be lucky to get a weekend in Brighton.

He must have picked up on her reluctance to answer personal questions as he moved back to why they were really meeting. "What genre is your novel?" he batted a fly away with his hand, "and do you have a title for it?"

"It's crime fiction. It's a working title really; I've gone with *Big Mistake*."

"As in it's a mistake someone has made, or a big mistake and someone may pay a price for their behaviour."

"More the second one I think."

She took another sip of her water. He didn't though.

He raised his eyebrows, "You could maybe do both angles. I like it though, it says a lot. Do you want to email me some of your chapters and I can read through them and give you some feedback?"

She could do. She'd set up a Gmail account so could remain fairly anonymous.

"If you're sure, I can easily do that."

Please . . . take a sip.

"Quite sure. Have you got your phone with you? I can give you my email."

She didn't want him seeing her phone. It was on silent but it had been vibrating as texts were coming through – the last thing she wanted was him seeing anything from Neil that might give the game away. She reached in her

113

bag for her phone, and lifted it slightly away from him, as if it was a poker hand she was hiding.

He reeled off his email and she typed it in. "Send those chapters and then perhaps we could meet again to discuss them. Does that sound okay?"

"Yes. Thank you. I'll forward you the chapters when I go back to my room."

He reached for the plastic cup and took a sip.

Hall-e-luj-ah!

Now all he needed to do was finish it and she could take both their cups to the bin and slip his in her bag. Then she was done with the whole fiasco.

"Good," he said, "and at least this way, we'll be doing a bit of mentoring. There's a lot going on with the busy timetable and you have paid, so you want to get some value for money while you're here. You'd get more from the variety of lectures, rather than spending too much time with me."

"Yes, it's certainly a packed programme."

"It is. Oh, and I'm not sure how good you are at general knowledge, but just to let you know, it seems we have been co-opted into a quiz group this evening."

"A quiz group?" she frowned. No way.

"Yeah, courtesy of Garth. Seemingly we're in a team with Paul, Verity and Norma. He thinks that with Paul and Norma being older, we'll have a head start."

She widened her eyes, "I like his style, but I'm not sure it's my scene." There was no way she was spending any more time than necessary with him. And very shortly, she'd have the cup so wouldn't need to. Job done as far as she was concerned.

"Me neither. I just agreed as it sounds a bit of a laugh."

"It certainly would be with me on the team," she shook her head, "my general knowledge is pretty dire. I'll have a word with Garth to count me out."

She gulped down the last of her water, hoping he'd do the same. But he didn't.

"Good luck with that. I know Garth, once he sets his mind on something, it's hard to budge him."

"So, you're definitely going?"

"It seems churlish not to, it's only a quiz. And seemingly we can take drinks in with us. So I can slowly sink into oblivion and won't give a jot about the questions."

Her antenna went up. Drinks meant glasses. And glasses meant his mouth would be round one. If she didn't get the plastic cup, there would be at least one more opportunity. But surely she could get the cup – she was so close. *Please, drink the rest of the bloody water.*

Someone whistling a tune caught her attention and she turned her head. Daryl was holding a tray and clearing the adjacent tables. If she wasn't mistaken, he was whistling to try and catch her attention to let her know he was there.

"Right," she stood up quickly. "I'll pop back to my room and email you those chapters."

Daryl moved towards the adjacent table and smiled at them both. "It's lovely out here, isn't it?"

"Mmmm, it is," she nodded. Concerned he might expose her by inferring something about why she was really there, she needed to get away. Screw the cup, unfortunately.

"What time did you say the quiz is tonight?" she asked Ed, feigning interest.

"Eight thirty. Have you decided to join in after all?"

"Why not? Although I might well be a silent participant," she grinned, "not because I'm rude, it's more I won't know the answers."

"You and me both, then. We'll sink into oblivion together, shall we?"

Her tummy fluttered but she didn't respond.

"I'm going to stay out here," he said pulling his glasses down onto his face, "and make some phone calls. It's too nice to be inside."

She picked up her empty plastic cup – his was still half full.

"Shall I take yours?"

"It's fine. I'll see to it. See you at lunch, maybe?"

"Okay," she nodded. She was too jittery in his company to join him for lunch. She needed a break from him. And to remind herself why she was there.

As she picked up her bag, he nodded and it hit her again how hot he was. It was easy to see why Sophie had been attracted to him in the first place with his dark expressive eyes, his hawkish nose, and manly, gritty stubble. His short hair was styled, no doubt by a top salon, and it had a wave to it and curled slightly at the ends rather like Colin Firth as Mr Darcy in Pride and

116

Prejudice. His physique was hot too – he was certainly all muscle and easy on the eye in his polo shirt, showing of his pecs. But she gave herself a shake; she'd never be sucked in by him. Her remit was to expose him and she was going to make sure she did for Sophie's sake. He needed to support his child. That was the only reason she was there masquerading as a would-be author. If that meant pretending to like the man, then so be it. She was only playing a part and it didn't matter what he looked like.

Once she had his DNA, she'd never have to see him again.

19.

The evening of the quiz, they were all seated around a circular table in one of the classrooms chatting about what fun name they could come up with to call their team, as they'd been asked to do.

Garth returned from the bar carrying a tray of drinks and placed them on the table. He shared them out amongst them, her, Verity, Norma, Paul and Ed. Even if she hadn't have wanted to participate in the quiz, she found herself well and truly shanghaied into it by Verity over dinner. But it was a means to an end she'd told herself as she got ready that evening and selected a pretty green dress which brought out the colour of her eyes. Not that she'd dressed nicely to get Ed's attention. She'd brought the dress with her and it made a change from wearing jeans. She wasn't about to put any makeup on, though – that would mean she was trying to impress, and she definitely wasn't.

The compere, a middle-aged lady, standing on a plinth at the front of the classroom, leaned into the microphone. "Five more minutes everyone, and we'll make a start. We'll do the first set of questions then take a short break to top up our glasses."

One of the men from an adjacent table called out "Hurray" which seemed to amuse many, judging by the sniggering. There appeared to be about twelve teams all seated around circular tables. Garth placed the tray against the wall next to his chair, "I'll keep this for the break to take the glasses back and top us up."

No you won't, she said to herself . . . I will. At the break, she would offer to buy the next round. That would give her the opportunity to collect the used glasses from the table, and then when she headed back to the bar with them, she could stop on the corridor and slip Ed's used glass into her bag. Easy peasy. She'd got the sterile bag ready to prevent it becoming contaminated. She felt more relaxed. If luck was on her side, she could well be on her way back to London in the morning.

There were six of them in their team. They seemed to have formed an informal group and she liked them all, with the exception of Ed. But she was mellowing and intended to act nice to get what she wanted. She raised her gin and tonic to her lips with her eyes on him as he took a sip of his pint. For some reason she was drawn to his Adam's apple as he swallowed. Everything about him was pleasing on the eye. His navy polo shirt fitted him like a glove, and the muscles on his bare arms tensed as he lifted the glass to his lips. And he smelled divine. All sharp, musky, and laden with spice.

"A list is coming round to jot your team name on," the compere said.

"Right folks," Garth picked up a pen, "what do you reckon? Something bookish and amusing maybe, I thought. How about Simple Minds?"

"That's very good," Paul laughed, "you've done this before, clearly."

Ed joined in, "Yes, he has mate, plenty of times. And he'll probably know all the answers as he's in a quiz league."

"I'm glad he's on our team then, and not the opposition."

"Come on," Gareth grinned, "there must be others. Anything better anyone?"

"I was thinking maybe No Idea," Paul suggested, "spelled as three words though and using e-y-e and d-e-a-r."

"I like that," Verity said. "I can't think of one. I'm rubbish at anything like this."

"What about Agatha Quiz-team?" Norma piped up.

"Hey, that's brilliant, Norma" Ruby giggled, and Verity joined in. "Absolutely brilliant."

Ed licked the beer moisture from his lips, "Yes, that is very good," he grinned with his lovely white teeth. Not Turkey teeth or anything crass like that; his were perfectly natural. For some bizarre reason Ruby thought about what sex might be like with him. It totally shocked her even thinking that way. All the time she was with Richie, sex was more something that happened at the end of an evening out, and certainly not something she particularly thought about. If she did, it was more as a chore. And she'd purposely kept busy at the weekends when he was home to avoid an afternoon frolicking.

"So it's unanimous?" Ed asked, "are we going for Agatha Quiz Team?"

They all nodded in agreement.

"Agatha Quiz Team it is then," Garth said reaching for the pen. "Am I chief scriber or does anyone else fancy it?"

"You go ahead," Verity smiled. And there was something about that smile. It wasn't a gushing, I fancy you type of smile, but it showed affection. In the space of a day and a half, they'd formed a pleasant little group. She must ask Verity about her own marriage, was she happy?

"Hey," Garth said, "while I've got you all here, don't forget tomorrow at two o'clock, you need to register your interest in Stage Shenanigans. I'll be there and I can swing it to make sure you are taking part in my play."

"Is that allowed?" Verity asked.

"Probably not," Garth laughed. "No, seriously, you can have your own friends take part if you want to. It's very informal. The audience vote on the best play and there's an award on the last night."

"What sort of award?"

"A tiny cup, so nothing major. But it's nice and gives the scriptwriters amongst us a chance to shine."

"I think it's great," Paul said, "I might have a go myself next year, I like the sound of it."

Ruby was taking it all in but had no intention of going. After tonight, all being well, she was out of there and back in her flat in London. All she needed was that glass Ed was drinking out of. Just an hour or so, and she'd be done. The summer school would be a distant dream she'd laugh about at work.

"Oh, and I forgot to say," Garth carried on, "If you're taking part in my play, the husband and the sister will have bad colds. All will be revealed tomorrow, but that's part of the script. So whoever takes part, will have to pretend to be bunged up with cold."

"Tissues to the ready then by the sound of things," Verity said.

Ruby took a breath in. Tissues would be a good Plan C, if she couldn't get Ed's beer glass. But she wasn't a defeatist – she was going to get it, come hell or high water.

"Okay, ladies and gentlemen, I've got all the names in, are we ready to make a start? Right, let's begin with question one. It's a music one. Who was the first woman ever to be inducted into the Rock and Roll Hall of Fame?"

Garth whispered, "I reckon Diana Ross. Anyone else?"

"Diana Ross sounds good to me," Verity said.

"Me too," Ruby agreed. She had no idea, but it sounded feasible. Diana Ross had been mega in her day.

"What about Aretha Franklin?" Ed chipped in.

"Hey, could be," Garth nodded.

"Could be either of them, I would have thought," Paul joined in.

"Ruby?" Garth asked.

"I think maybe Aretha Franklin." She had no idea really but just knew somehow that Ed would be right.

"Then let's go with Aretha Franklin," Norma said, "I have a feeling it might be her."

"Righto, Aretha it is," Garth said, filling the name in on the answer sheet.

"Quiet now," the compere said. "Question two, this is on history. Who found the lost city of Machu Picchu, the lost city of the Inca's in 1911?"

Paul screwed his face up. "I read a book about this years ago. I think it might have been erm . . . Manco Cápac? I have no idea why that name has stuck with me. Or maybe he's a legend figure? I'm not entirely sure."

Ruby cleared her throat. "It's Hiram Bingham. Manco Cápac was the mythical founder of the Inca Empire."

"You're sure?" Gareth challenged.

"Quite sure."

"How do you know?" Ed asked.

"I know a bit about it as I've been there with my parents."

Verity widened her eyes. "Really? How fantastic. I bet that was an amazing experience."

The questions carried on and Ruby surprised herself joining in. Maybe she just got lucky, but she liked that she could answer a few. Ed was watching her intensely which made her feel on edge. But she was enjoying herself and for a while completely forgot about the task ahead. Ed knew several of the answers, and she had an inkling he knew more than he was letting on, but was sometimes being vague to give the others a turn.

123

"Last question before we take a break. We always end with a fun question. Here goes . . . Bridget Jones, is famous for her *granny* what?"

"Knickers," Norma said confidently. "I love that movie."

Verity chuckled. "I wouldn't be without my granny knickers."

Ruby laughed, too, but Ed didn't. His eyes were on her. She thought of the thong she was wearing and wondered if Ed was wondering what knickers she had on – a strange thought to have but she felt herself blushing again.

"Okay, everyone," the compere said, "that's it for round one. It's time to take a break and top up our glasses." She checked her watch. "Let's be back in here for nine-thirty and we'll do the second round and the mark the questions. I have a carrier bag of goodies for the winning team."

Before the compere had even finished her spiel, Ruby had reached for the tray propped up against the wall. This was her moment. She was having Ed's glass come what may.

"What is everyone drinking?" she asked standing up, "my shout." She reached for Ed's empty beer glass first and placed it to the left corner of the tray. Paul picked up Norma's glass and his own and placed them on the tray. "That's kind of you Ruby, I'll have a glass of house red – only a small one, mind."

"I think I will too," Norma said.

"Another Stella for me," Garth placed his glass on the tray, "thank you."

Ed stood up and reached forward with both his hands to take the tray from her, "Allow me. I'll come with you."

God no. That was the last thing she wanted. She could hardly put his glass in her bag with him there.

"I'm fine, honestly." She kept tight hold of the tray. But he held on equally as firmly to it. They must have appeared like a comedy act, but she wasn't letting go.

"Please, allow me," he looked directly in her eyes, "I'd rather get them." She knew he was being chivalrous, but she needed the glass.

As he pulled the tray towards himself, she should have let it go. But she didn't. She held on tightly, almost pulling it out of his hands. It felt like slow motion as she watched his pint glass wobble. It wasn't a traditional pint glass, it was more elegant and widened at the top, with a narrow bottom, therefore empty, it wasn't stable.

"Oooh, steady," Norma called out. The glass toppled. Ruby let go of the tray Ed was holding to try and catch it, but she was too late, she missed it. All eyes around the table watched the glass fall to the floor and shatter into pieces. Many of the crowd clapped and cheered.

"Oh, no!" Ruby cried.

Gareth jumped up, "It's okay, be careful Ruby. I'll get a dustpan," he started to move the chairs to one side, "don't you worry."

"Are you sure?" she was mortified, not because a glass had broken – accidents happen, it was because her Plan C was in pieces, literally. "I can sweep it up."

"No, honestly, you get the drinks with Ed, that's the most important thing," he winked. "I'll have this sorted by the time you get back."

She walked beside Ed and they made their way towards the bar. There was no going home tomorrow now, not when she had zilch.

"The quiz is a bit of a laugh if nothing else, isn't it?" he said as they walked side by side along the corridor with him carrying the tray.

Oh yeah, a real laugh. It might be for him. Why couldn't he just have let her go to the bar on her own? She'd have the glass in her bag now and be packing up to leave.

"Yeah, I suppose it is. I'm just not quick enough to think of the answers."

"Get away with you, you did well. I was impressed."

"Thanks," she said, then added, "you were pretty hot yourself," realising again that she should think before speaking.

Ed laughed.

But Ruby wasn't laughing.

Her focus was on being thwarted three times – the toothbrush, the paper cup and now his beer glass. Now what could she do? Neil was going to go mad.

"Will you excuse me," she said as they reached the bar.

"I'll still be here when you come back, I'm sure," he said nodding to the queue in front of him.

"Can you remember what everyone's having?"

"I think so. Any particular gin for you? Do you like flavoured ones?"

"Gordon's is fine, thanks. I'll be back in a tick."

As she made her way to the bathroom, she was aware of an internal conflict rising up inside her. And it was definitely not something she was used to experiencing around men. But she couldn't deny it was happening currently around Ed. Something had shifted significantly during the quiz. It wasn't anything she could explore, or act upon even if she wanted to. He was a serial scoundrel of the highest degree leaving her friend high and dry to bring up his baby with no support whatsoever. No . . . she couldn't possibly be attracted to him, she just couldn't.

She splashed cold water on her face. The evening had meant to be a light-hearted bit of fun, but wished she'd never taken part. Feelings she didn't want, nor had any inclination to act upon, had surfaced and she needed to stifle them quick.

Damn the bloody Agatha Quiz-Team.

***

He couldn't help but watch her as she walked away – everything about her appealed. It was as if her presence enveloped him and despite his deep suspicion about her motives for being there, he found himself warming to her. She was clearly no dummy, either. She was bright. He loved her giddy excitement over the questions during the quiz, her infectious giggle was cute. It was only with the others though, not him. Her wariness around him and avoidance of meeting his eyes unless it was necessary, was a reminder to him that she had an agenda – he just wasn't sure what it was. He'd done more research on the newspaper she worked at, but gleaned nothing. Why was she posing as an admin assistant attending a writer's school? And most surprising, the first three chapters of her novel she'd emailed were good. If he was totally honest, her indifference irked him. Women coming onto him he was used to, but she kept her distance. And when she did engage with him, he felt it was put on. As if she had to be nice to him. Even her red hair, which she was currently wearing loose, cascading around her shoulders and down her back, was growing on him, despite normally steering clear of red haired women.

He'd rather liked it though when she blushed. As she'd done when she said he was hot, though he knew she meant hot in answering questions, but it made him feel good. She looked pretty hot herself in that green dress. And who knew, she might even be wearing granny knickers. In his mind, she peeled off her dress, revealing big knickers. It made him smile.

But before he got too carried away, he needed to find out why she was there. But how? He couldn't just come out and challenge her, much as he'd like to. No, he had

128

to bide his time and be nice. And keep the shower on cool to stop his body betraying him.

The queue had barely moved before he saw her making her way back the bar. Her expression altered as she was intercepted by Daryl. Whatever was he saying to her? If Daryl didn't realise she didn't like him, he must be pretty thick. Her body language spoke volumes, he wasn't getting a look in. She said something which seemed to pacify him as he nodded and walked away. Returning to the bar, she looked exactly the same as before. No lipstick, in fact very little makeup at all. In his experience, women seemed to be fixated on their appearance. All the cosmetic enhancement stuff turned him off, especially the Botox and pumped up lips. Ruby had none of those – she didn't need them. She was a naturally beautiful woman. He saw men looking at her, yet she didn't seem to notice. But then again, he needed to remember, she was an expert at deception. Wasn't she deceiving them all by portraying herself as a novice writer when in fact she was a journalist?

"Can I help you?" the barmaid interrupted his thoughts. He gave their order.

"Just getting served now," he said as Ruby stood next to him.

She reached in her bag for her purse, "I'd like to get these."

"No need," he shook his head.

"But I said I would."

"I know you did. But I'd rather you saved your money, London's not a cheap place to live."

"You're right about that, but I like to pay my way."

"Another time then maybe," he tapped his card on the machine, placed the glasses on the tray and picked it up to head back to the quiz. She fell into step beside him.

"Do you know what sessions you're attending tomorrow?" he asked.

"Yours first thing, then I thought, erm . . . Romantic Fiction looked interesting."

"Sounds good. You like romantic fiction, do you?"

"Sometimes. I like romcom as it's not too heavy. If I don't read for a couple of days, it's easy to pick it back up again and be straight in there."

"Yes, easier than trying to remember clues to particular plots."

"Exactly."

Why wasn't she asking him questions? If she was there to find out more about him, surely she should be quizzing him. She had ample opportunity to do so when they met outside. Yet all she'd asked was where he used to live in the UK. He didn't get it. He hated mystery of any kind. He wanted to know more about her. And if he was totally honest, the caveman in him wanted to pick her up, throw her over his shoulder and hoist her off to bed.

Down boy, he thought, then imagined her again wearing nothing but granny knickers, which caused him to chuckle.

130

"What's funny?" she asked, "something's amusing you."

He thought quickly. "I was trying to think of a strategy to get out of taking part in Garth's play, then pictured him whining about it."

"Ah, I see. Do you know what, I reckon it might be quite fun."

"Really? You're thinking of taking part?"

"I'm not sure," she turned to him with what he thought was a bit of a glint in her eye. "Maybe I will if you will." Surely she wasn't flirting – that wasn't her at all. Not with him anyway. What was this woman up to? She'd been very clear at dinner the previous evening she wasn't taking part in the play. Why the sudden change?

"Put like that then, I'll have to consider it."

She held the classroom door open for him and he carried the tray back to the table.

He definitely would be taking part now. Whatever it took, he was going to find out what the intriguing Ruby Lowe was up to.

21.

"There you bloody well are," Neil barked down the phone, "are you deliberately avoiding my calls? You are supposed to be bloody working in case you've forgotten."

Ruby sighed. "How could I forget with you ringing all the time?"

"I wouldn't need to if you got what you're supposed to. What's the bloody delay? We're all on standby here waiting to hear that you've got something to test."

"Yes, well it's easier said than done."

"Why? What's so difficult? Can't you get into his room?"

"No, I can't. It's guarded like a bank. He's specifically requested his privacy."

"Can't you use a more *innovative* approach?"

"If by *innovative* you mean going to his room with him, forget it. I've told you I'm not doing that."

"So, what's your plan then, because I'm warning you Ruby, don't come back without anything."

"Look, I am doing my best. But De'Ath's not stupid. I have to be careful. And who the hell is this Daryl character that thinks I owe him?"

"A nobody."

"Well, he might be a nobody to you – to me, he's a bleeding creep. He's threatening to grass me up to De'Ath."

"What! Who the bloody hell does he think he bloody well is?"

"God's gift to women, that's what. I'm sick to death of avoiding him."

"What the bloody hell is he after?"

"What do you think? He's flowering it up as just a drink, but I can assure you a drink isn't the only thing on his mind. He's got another agenda."

"All the more reason for you to get the hell out of there before De'Ath finds out."

"Yes, and I would if I could. I'm hoping today I might be onto something."

"Why, what's happening today?"

"Rehearsals for a play. I reckon I may be able to get some used tissues from De'Ath."

"Rehearsals for a bloody play? Used tissues? What are you talking about? You're not there on some bloody jolly, you know."

"Do you think I don't know that," she snapped. "Would you like to be on a stage with everyone watching while you act out a part?"

"No, I can't say I would."

"Exactly, and I don't want to either. I know I need something from De'Ath but I can't get near the bloke, I've tried, truly I have."

"Well, you're gonna have to try harder and do whatever you bloody well have to. You know the importance of this, we need something."

"Oh, don't I just."

"What about a glass he's used?"

"Believe you me, I have tried."

"You need to try harder then."

She raised her voice, "I am trying. Surely you can see how odd it would look if I reached for the glass he'd had his chops round and stuck it in my handbag."

She heard him sigh, "You have to get something, Ruby, the paper needs this story."

"I know. Look, I'm doing the best I can but if I can't get anything, then I may have to come back without."

"I'm warning you, don't do that."

"And I'm warning you, this is hard. I have to be careful, he's no dummy. He could smell a rat a mile away."

"Jesus bloody Christ. Only you could make things so bloody complicated. I wish I'd sent Millicent now."

"I wish you had, too. Look, I can only keep trying. Now, I'm going to have to go . . . preparation for my performance and all that. I'll let you know as soon as I have something."

"Okay, make sure you do. And . . . what is it they say, break a bloody leg!"

"Ha, ha very funny."

Ruby made her way towards the main hall with heaviness in the pit of her stomach. There were a number of people in groups chatting and clutching crib sheets. Ed was standing in a corner chatting to Verity and Garth. She made her way towards them.

"Here you are," Verity said with a smile.

"Sorry, I got held up on a phone call."

"Well, at least you're here now, I didn't fancy being on my own. I'm a bit nervous actually, I've never done anything like this before, have you?"

She wanted to blurt out yes, she had – in fact she was quite an accomplished actress.

"No, never, it'll certainly take me out of my comfort zone."

She smiled at Ed and Garth. Ed, looking as handsome as ever in his pristine shirt, with the ubiquitous logo on the pocket. Even his black jeans looked like he was modelling them. Obviously quality, no doubt with a designer label attached to them. How was it he could make a plain white shirt look so good?

"You're okay about it all?" Ed asked. Anyone would think he cared.

"Yeah, I'm fine. It's only a five-minute play, isn't it? And didn't you say Garth we'd have our lines in front of us?"

"That's right." Garth handed them a sheet with the play written on it. He'd used colours to highlight their speaking parts, the husband was in blue, the wife in red, and the sister in green.

"You'll see the first scene is the husband arguing with the wife, accusing her of having an affair."

They glanced down at the script. "You, Ruby, won't be on the stage during the argument."

She nodded.

"Ed, as the husband, you need to take on the persona of a man full of cold. So, you need to be quite nasal. You know, reading your lines through your nose. And several times, take the tissue out of your pocket and fake sneeze into it."

Ruby needed to get that tissue. No point in worrying it wouldn't be a real sneeze, or whether it would contain enough saliva to test his DNA, that wasn't her problem, getting the tissue was. But knowing how difficult it had been so far to get anything of his, and knowing her luck, he'd bring his own blinking handkerchief.

"Do you need me to go and fetch some tissues from my room?" Ruby asked hopefully.

Garth shook his head. "We don't need any props yet. We're just getting in positions and looking over the script. On Thursday we'll do a proper run through so we'll need them then, if you don't mind bringing some."

"Fine, leave it with me."

"Thanks. Right, the opening scene is the wife stood by the baby's crib rocking it gently. So, Verity, you're the wife. Ed, you're the husband, and you Ruby, you're the wife's sister. The husband starts a row with his wife suggesting that a neighbour has told him she'd been having an affair and that the baby might not be his. You'll see that the opening is them both rowing – the wife having a clever response to the allegations. There are a few witty sentences in there, if I say so myself," he stroked a pretend lapel. "So, we have the comedic argument between the two of them, the husband accusing, and the wife standing her ground. During the course of them rowing, the baby will start to cry – I've got a recording on my phone so I'll play that. The wife insists that of course the baby is his, then the sister," he looked at her, "that's you, Ruby, enters and says the baby is crying and heads towards the crib, lifting the doll out. You read the line about the baby feeling warm and may have a temperature, so you promptly remove the shawl and the audience can see the baby is black. Then it's you Ed, reading from the script. Ah-ha, I knew it. You've been sleeping with Freeman next door. The wife turns the tables on the husband and says she only has done because he's been neglecting her and she knows he's been having an affair too."

"Erm . . . sorry to interrupt," Verity said, "I'm not sure about the black doll. Do you think some people might take offense? I know it proves that the wife had been having an affair, and I get it's the comedy factor, but you know how things are right now, we need to be careful."

"I take your point," Garth said, "but the laughs aren't about the black baby, it's the fact that the husband was right all along."

"Okay." Verity didn't look convinced whereas Ruby wasn't one bit interested in the doll's colour upsetting the audience, her agenda was much more important.

"Ruby's watching them both as they argue, and finally Ed sneezes and asks, Right then, who in God's name am

I supposed to be having an affair with, he blows his nose. Who? At that moment, you, Ruby let out an enormous sneeze which I hope will amuse the audience. The wife looks at one and then the other, picks the baby up and says to you Ed, if you want her dumb sister, then you're welcome to her. You're both well suited, two thick dimwits together. She exits the stage, leaving you, Ed and Ruby on the stage. You, Ed say, I knew something wasn't right but I couldn't put my finger on it. But now I know for sure the baby isn't mine.

"Then, Ruby ends on the last line. I don't understand, how do you know for sure the baby isn't yours? Cue the audience laughing and applause."

He turned to Ed. "You okay with it all, Ed?"

"It looks good," he smiled. "It's light-hearted, which is what you're aiming for. I think you've done well."

"Thanks. And don't forget," Garth said, "after every line you deliver, you need to blow your nose. That's the whole premise of the play."

"Hey, I've just thought," Ruby said, "I'll bring a bag to dispose of the tissues after the play has finished." Garth frowned and gave her a quizzical look.

"You know, with all this Covid business, we need to dispose of the tissues properly."

"Yeah . . . sure . . . good idea. I'll leave that with you then, Ruby."

She nodded. It didn't matter to her he was condescending; all she was bothered about was how she could separate Ed's tissue from hers.

"So," Garth continued, "take the script away with you. You don't have to learn the lines as such, you'll be reading from the sheets, but as long as you know the basic plot. I'm hoping the audience will love it. They get quite carried away with Stage Shenanigans. It's a highlight of the week and a real laugh."

Oh, yeah, she could see that. With a bit of luck, if all went according to plan, she'd be laughing all the way back to London with snotty tissues in her pocket.

And at least then she'd hang on to her job.

22.

Ed had suggested they meet by the lake for feedback on the chapters she'd sent him. It certainly wasn't her preferred place to meet, it seemed too intimate, but she found herself agreeing. He had a persuasive way about him – that's what she put it down to, refusing to acknowledge she'd quite like to spend some time with him. As she turned past the accommodation block, she was relieved to see other delegates walking around the lake and occupying some of the benches – it felt less intimate. In the distance she could hear someone strumming a guitar, which was quite lovely.

"Hi," she said as she approached him sitting on a bench. Seeing him waiting for her, accelerated her heart and a weird feeling of excitement kicked in. He was wearing khaki shorts, a light blue tee-shirt, and the sexy shades – if she was totally honest, he looked incredibly hot. Not that she was going anywhere near that. Her poor friend had dallied, and had more than a good night of sex to remember him by.

"Hi," he stood up. "I wasn't sure if you wanted to sit here, or go for a walk?"

"A walk might be nice, if you're happy to."

"Yeah, definitely. I sit all day, so any chances I get to move about, I take them."

His phone started to ring but he ignored it. They set off walking towards the lake, the butterflies in her tummy were circulating. But she told herself it was because she was nervous about his review of her writing. It couldn't be anything else – she didn't like the man. But she had to admit, as she was getting ready to meet him, she had made a bit of an effort with her appearance. Not too flashy or anything, but cut-off blue jeans that showed off her ankles, and a tightly fitted white tee-shirt.

"Right," he said, as he let her go first where the path narrowed slightly, "the chapters."

"Oh, dear," she pulled a face, "should I have taken the seat after all?"

"Not at all, they're really good. You have an engaging style of writing."

Her faced flushed, she hadn't expected that at all. "I bet you say that to anyone who asks you to look at their work."

"Nope," he shook his head, "sometimes I see little potential, but I certainly can see plenty with yours. I've made some comments, which I'll email back to you, but they are just suggestions, you don't have to use them."

"Of course I'd use them. Why wouldn't I? You're a bestselling author and I'm a . . . an admin clerk."

"Well, I would hope that I've learnt a lot myself along the way. I haven't always been proficient though, far from it. In the early days, I had my share of rejections."

"Gosh, that's hard to imagine."

"It's true, believe you me, I've had plenty. But one day I got lucky and the rest is history. And you might too. I was wondering, have you done any creative writing courses? You have a great flair for scene setting, it's hard to imagine you're a novice."

"No," she quickly dismissed, "I haven't." If he only knew she was a journalist and spent three years at university studying writing. Did he know something? He couldn't, surely? Not unless Daryl had spilled the beans but that seemed unlikely. If that had been the case, Ed would be the type to confront her. No, she was confident he didn't know anything. But she hated lying and quickly moved on. "I'm not sure what I'll do with the manuscript once it's finished."

"You can always go down the independent publishing route, but you're quite a way from that at the moment. You will need to work with an editor."

Yeah, right. As if she would ever afford one of those.

He carried on. "Something I read once in my early days of writing which I think might help is, never use two words when one will do. And I think that applies to your chapters, you can still get the vital message across, but in less words. You don't need to memorise any of this, I'll give prompts in the email. But say I was to write . . . *It doesn't matter what kind of coffee I buy, where it's from, or if it's organic or not, I need to have cream because I really don't like how the bitterness makes me feel.* That's a mouthful and far too long and complicated, with extra words that are superfluous. Now if I was to write, *I add cream to my coffee because the bitter taste makes me feel unwell* – it says the same in half the words, making it clearer and easier for the reader.

She listened to his voice, it was infectious. Once he'd shortened the sentence, she could see immediately it was better. It demonstrated that even as a journalist, creative writing was a completely different style to factual reporting.

"You can see what I'm getting at, less is more."

"Yes, I see that."

"And remember, easy reading is damn hard writing."

She grinned, "I like that."

"Me too. It speaks volumes, doesn't it?"

"Yes, it does."

His phone rang again.

"Why don't you get it? It might be urgent."

He took the phone out of his pocket, glanced at the screen and pressed accept. "Hi Carolyn."

Carolyn? Was that his girlfriend? Her tummy clenched. She knew he was a widow as Verity had said, but she'd not envisaged he had a girlfriend, possibly because when he spoke, it always sounded like he was on his own. She moved away to give him some privacy, unsure whether or not to leave.

He was quiet, listening to whatever the caller was saying before he responded. "Right, you'll need to get me on a flight, then."

Flight? Something was wrong if he had to leave. She gestured with her hand she was going back to the accommodation so he could have some privacy. "Just a minute, Carolyn," he said to the caller.

"I'll catch you later," Ruby said.

He screwed up his face, "I'm sorry about this, a bit of an emergency."

"It's fine. No probs," she nodded and walked away. If he was leaving, then she would be too. And Neil couldn't be mad with her – it wouldn't be her fault he'd left early. It'd actually be a win win all round if he did go. It'd be better for everyone. So why had a wave of sadness hit her? – followed by a thud of reality that she didn't want him to go.

After returning to her room to shower and change for dinner, she selected a white knee length skirt and a cute pink top and, looking at herself in the mirror, was pleased with her appearance. Ed was supposed to be the after dinner speaker that evening in the main hall and she was looking forward to it. Despite her resistance to him, she could see his appeal. He had bucket loads of charisma when he was being nice. Would he be leaving the following day, or the day after? Whichever, it saddened her, which was surprising considering how she initially couldn't stand the man.

As she made her way through the accommodation block, Daryl was loitering by the entrance doors as she came out, smoking a cigarette. Her tummy tightened. She needed to pacify him, she had no choice.

"Hello," he exhaled a puff of smoke and extinguished the butt on the wall ashtray. "I was hoping to catch you."

"What for?"

"You know what for. Anyone would think you were avoiding me."

"I've been busy."

"Busy fawning around Mr Millionaire? If only he knew who you were, eh? I wonder what he'd make of that?"

"And I wonder what my boss would make of you pestering me."

"Pestering you?" he scowled, "I don't think so. I'm just being friendly and only want a chance to buy you a drink. But you keep stalling . . . so how about now?"

"I can't now. I've arranged a one to one with . . . Ed De'Ath."

"What, as part of the fake mentoring? How about tomorrow then? It's the fancy dress. I'm sure you'll be free sometime then?"

"Okay."

"Good, I'll look forward to it. Shall we say eight thirty in the bar?"

"Fine, I'll see you then." She attempted to move away but he caught her arm. "I can't wait to see what you're dressing up as."

"Hi," Verity approached. "Sorry to interrupt. I'm heading for the bar, can I get you one in, Ruby?"

"It's okay, I'll come with you," Ruby said, grateful for the reprieve.

"Are you sure?" Verity looked apologetic; "I didn't mean to interrupt."

"You're not interrupting at all." She linked her arm through her friend's, "See you later then," she said to Daryl as they headed towards the bar. If it kept him quiet, then she'd have one drink with him. The whole fiasco was becoming a nightmare. As if it wasn't bad enough trying to get something from Ed, Daryl was an added complication. She doubted he would say anything, he'd have no leverage then, but she couldn't risk him exposing her. She'd stalled him long enough; tomorrow she'd have to have a drink with him, but it'd be just the one, he made her flesh crawl. And if Ed was leaving, then she'd be out of there too, so the drink might not happen at all.

"What was he after?" Verity whispered when they were well away from Daryl.

"He wants me to have a drink with him."

"Ah, I guessed as much. I hope I didn't really interrupt. I thought you didn't look comfortable with him."

"You did right. No, he's definitely not my type."

"Who is your type?"

"I don't know really," Ruby shrugged, "certainly someone the complete opposite of him."

"Like a certain writer speaking tonight?"

"What?" Ruby felt her cheeks warming, "No, of course not. Whatever makes you think that?"

"Because of the chemistry between you both. He barely takes his eyes off you. You must have noticed, surely?"

"No," Ruby shook her head, "I can't say I have."

"Really?" Verity raised an eyebrow, "Do you know your nose is growing longer by the minute."

23.

It was the night of the fancy dress party. Ed was standing at the bar with Jocelyn and Garth who both looked splendid in their fancy dress costumes. Jocelyn was dressed as Snow White and Garth as a pirate with a fetching red coat, and a plastic cutlass strapped around his waist.

Judging by the early turnout, everyone had made a great effort. The bar area was alive with Disney characters, and sixties and seventies music was blaring out from the disco set up in the adjacent conservatory. People were in high spirits but Ed's mind was on his brother, Michael. Carolyn, on his instruction, has approved payment for four weeks in a drug rehabilitation clinic in the US which he'd been in before. It had worked with him two years ago; he'd been clean since then as far as Ed was aware, so he was hopeful it would work again. He'd explained the situation to Garth about his brother and him having to leave to head to Heathrow for a flight home after his final teaching session, therefore he would miss Stage Shenanigans. Garth was sympathetic and co-opted Myles, who'd joined them for dinner on the first evening of the White Badgers, to take his part in the play.

Ed had made a bit of an effort. The theme had been *Once-upon-a-time,* so the scope was endless. He was wearing a white shirt with a frill down the front and around the sleeves, a pair of black jodhpurs, a military-style jacket as that's all he had, and long black boots. Even though he was concerned about his errant brother, he found himself buzzing, anticipating the arrival of Ruby. He'd overheard her earlier saying she had a costume, and on the one hand he felt like a horny schoolboy waiting to see her; there was certainly something about her that attracted him, and he couldn't help imagining her dressed as Little Red Riding Hood, with her gorgeous red hair it would be the perfect choice. But on the other hand, she obviously had an agenda. She's a journalist yet she never asked him a single question. It puzzled him and he didn't like puzzles.

"There you go," he handed Jocelyn a glass of Pinot Grigio. She looked striking dressed as Snow White, although a bit heavy on the makeup front. He passed Garth a beer. His mate looked impressive wearing his Cavalier hat with a plume and his black curly wig.

"It's quite a turnout, people have really gone to town," he said to Jocelyn.

"Oh, they always do. Fancy dress is one of the highlights of the week."

Ed smiled, "Yeah, I can see. I like the contrast between the daily academic sessions and the evening events. You've done a great job with the programme."

"Thank you." Jocelyn gave a self-confident smile. "Be sure to put that in your evaluation, won't you?"

"Of course I will."

"Oh look," Garth nodded towards the door, "here's Verity and Ruby now."

Ed's eyes were drawn towards the entrance. Verity looked like she was dressed as Snow White as well, but it wasn't her that had his attention. Ruby looked stunning, even though stunning didn't come close to describing her. Each time he saw her, he appreciated her physical attributes, but her transformation in the fancy dress outfit was nothing short of . . . spectacular. She hadn't gone for the Little Red Riding Hood look. She'd come as a mermaid, but not just any mermaid, with her gorgeous red hair cascading down her back, this was Ariel. The full length turquoise fitted skirt emphasised her small waist and covered her long legs. The legs he'd fantasised being wrapped around him. The skirt material had scales on it and tapered at her ankles. Tiny black pumps covered her delicate feet and he could see a glimpse of skin around her ankles. As if the skirt didn't do enough for his libido, the purple crop top which clung provocatively to her perfectly formed breasts, was incredibly arousing. The sheer wrap she wore around her shoulders might have partially covered the top, but nowhere near enough – her flat abdomen was still peeking out. Prickles of heat ran through him. She looked like a goddess. He took a huge swig of his pint. It was going to be a long night.

Those hot tingles kept on coming over dinner. They seemed to be seated at the same table most evenings, the little group they'd formed on the first evening had continued.

The visceral stab of desire that engulfed him when he'd first set eyes on her that evening, showed no sign of abating. Ruby was sat on the opposite side of the table to him and Garth. She was flanked by Verity and Jocelyn – two Snow Whites. The two women had laughed when they saw each other, but he knew they were pissed off, each vying to be the best Snow White. It made the scene before him all the more headier – Ariel, the gorgeous mermaid, sat in the middle, as if the Snow Whites were her guardians. The more he looked at her, the more beautiful she became. He took a swig of his third pint. Beer goggles were known for making women appear more attractive to the tipsy eye – Verity and Jocelyn were proof of that, both Snow Whites now quite alluring. But when the woman you've been staring at all evening is already gorgeous, those beer goggles are like a shot in the arm – or maybe the groin. He glanced away and forked up some of his chicken curry, while in his mind, he was throwing the flapping mermaid over his shoulder and carrying to his bed.

"You're quiet," Paul said, "this sort of evening not for you?"

"No, no, it's all good," he said, "I think it's great to see everyone dressed up. It's just I've got a lot on my mind, work stuff, nothing to worry about."

"Well, forget that for now, you're here to have a good time. Work will still be there waiting once you've had some well deserved fun."

Fun, Ed thought, Ruby now naked on his bed. Oh what fun that would be. "You're absolutely right."

Jocelyn poured her and Ruby some water, "I must say, your outfit looks pretty impressive, Ruby. Do you go to a lot of fancy dress events?"

"God, no. But as luck would have it, I went to one a couple of months ago with . . . erm," a wave of sadness passed across her face, "and I wore this, so I thought I might as well get the use out of it a second time."

"Well, you look absolutely stunning," Jocelyn said taking a sip of water, "if there are any single men here, they are going to be requesting a dance with you tonight, that's for sure."

Ruby smiled, showing off her perfect white teeth. "I can't imagine there are an abundance of single men here, and with it being a disco, I doubt there'd be any opportunities for smoochy dances."

Now Ed was dancing with Ruby. She was grinding against him, the dance floor a blur...

"Good evening," Daryl approached the table, "I hope you're all enjoying dinner?"

They all said yes, except Ruby – she said nothing.

Nothing came from those lips because they were too busy pressed up against his...

"Sorry to interrupt," Daryl's eyes focussed on Ruby, "just to let you know, I've got us a table in the bar for our drink after you've finished eating."

What the hell? Ed ran cold at his words. He didn't like the sound of this.

And he could tell by the brief nod Ruby gave him, she wasn't at all enthusiastic. The knot of rope inside him tightened. Why was she having a drink with Daryl of all people? Something was off here; it had to be. It felt like his princess had suddenly been wrenched from his grasp.

24.

Ruby's tummy was churning as she approached Daryl's table. She had little choice but to try and pacify him, but regretted coming as she pulled out the chair opposite him and saw desire dancing in his lecherous eyes. Sitting down, she tightened her wrap around herself, as if that would somehow protect her.

"You look stunning, Ruby," he said. "I've got you a G&T; I noticed that's your tipple."

"Thank you. Shouldn't you be working?"

"I am allowed time off you know."

"Wouldn't you rather be spending it away from here?"

"No. I'd rather find out more about you."

"Well, I'm afraid you're likely to be disappointed, there isn't much to tell."

"I'll be the judge of that." He reached out and stroked a finger along her forearm. She pulled her arm away. "Don't do that!"

"Why? What's wrong?"

"I barely know you."

"I know you don't, that's why we're here, so you can get to know me."

She took a sip of her drink. She needed to choose her words carefully so he didn't sprag on her to Ed. "There's no point in that, as I'm leaving soon and heading back to . . . home."

"I know that, but it doesn't stop us having a bit of fun while you're here."

"I think you've got the wrong idea about me," another sip of gin for courage, "I have a boyfriend at home," she lied, "who wouldn't be very pleased to hear you talking to me like that."

"Well, I won't tell him if you won't," he said with a grin.

Ruby shuddered. "Look," she tried to inject a bit of sympathy into her expression, "I don't mean to be awful, but I don't know what you think is happening here, so I need to be clear. I'm not interested in you."

"Why are you here, then?"

"Because you threatened me."

He widened his eyes, "I don't think I did."

"Okay, well you indicated that you'd say about the winning ticket for the mentorship."

"Ah, yeah that. What's that all about? Why did you need that ticket? Are you after hooking up with a multi-millionaire?"

"No."

"Then why was I paid to facilitate it?"

"I have no idea. Who actually paid you?"

"Who do you think? Your boss."

"And how do you know him?"

"I don't. It was through a third party. Besides, who cares about that? You're here and I'm here, we're both adults, and I am really attracted to you. Maybe we can continue this conversation in my room?"

She shook her head. "Nothing is going to happen between us. I've never been into casual relationships. So, I am sorry you thought otherwise." She glanced at her watch, "I think it'd be best if I made a move."

He grabbed her arm, "Not yet you don't. You owe me, remember."

"I don't owe you . . ."

"Oh yes you do, little mermaid." His grip tightened. "Let's go to my room, an hour of fun, and then I'll leave you alone."

"You're hurting me," she said, trying to pull from his grip.

"I bet you like it rough," he said, his eyes dark with lust, "I promise you won't be disappointed."

"There you are, Ruby," Ed stopped at the table looking all gallant in black, like a musketeer. "Are you ready for that dance you promised me?"

Daryl let go of her arm. "Do you fucking mind," he hissed. "We're having a private conversation here."

"Yeah, I gathered that," Ed said. "It's just that Ruby had promised," he turned to her, "you're popular this evening, two men fighting over you." He smiled politely at Daryl, "I hope it doesn't become fisticuffs at dawn!" It was an obvious warning.

Never was Ruby more pleased to see Ed. She jumped up, eager to get away.

Ed held out his hand and she willingly grasped it. She wanted to kiss him for saving her. "I think a dance would be lovely, thank you." She turned to Daryl, "Thanks for the drink."

Daryl's eyes darkened. He turned to Ed, "Before you go . . ." Ruby knew by his smug face he was going to expose her. "It's not you she's interested in . . . it's who you are." He glared at her, "Why don't you tell him you're a reporter, here to get the lowdown on him?"

Ed didn't even stiffen. If he was surprised, he didn't show it. He kept hold of her hand and spoke to Daryl. "Yeah, don't I know it. Shame you've spilled the beans though, I was enjoying the covert interrogation." He turned and winked at her, "Ready for that dance?"

Ed's hand held hers firmly as he led her past the conservatory disco and outside into the gardens. Although grateful for being saved, she felt like a naughty schoolgirl being led to the headmaster's office for a bollocking.

The game was well and truly up.

25.

Ed didn't let go of her hand as they exited the main building and made their way past the outside seating area, across the neatly manicured lawns to a small, intimate gazebo in a secluded area. The disco music was much quieter but still blaring out seventies favourites.

"Here," he took off his long, woollen coat and wrapped it around her, "let's sit for a minute, shall we?" Her tummy was in a turmoil, not only because she'd been exposed, but also because he was looking incredibly sexy in the Pride and Prejudice getup.

"So . . ." his enquiring eyes looked directly into hers, "I'm guessing that creep was intending to keep your secret if you were nice to him?"

"Yeah," she nodded, "something like that."

"Is anything worth putting up with a dickhead like him?"

The truth wasn't an option; it would give the game away. Fine, he knew she was a journalist, but no more than that.

"Clearly you don't like the man," he continued, "that's obvious. Every time I've seen you with him, you've seemed a little . . . tense."

She wasn't answering anything that might incriminate her further. It was much better to keep quiet and say as little as possible. But she was curious about one thing.

"Did you really know who I was before Daryl told you, or did you make that up?"

"I already knew."

"How?"

"I had you checked out. Don't worry," he said, "nothing intrusive. I knew that mentorship farce wasn't right. It was easy enough for my PA to find out you worked for the Northfield Reporter."

He'd known all along – but not everything. He couldn't find out the real truth – according to Neil, this was her last chance. She had to keep her job, even though there was little chance of getting anything of his now, anyway. And if she was totally honest, did she really want to? He was decent . . . then she remembered to correct herself. He wasn't decent – if he was, he'd acknowledge his responsibilities to his child. Yet, despite knowing all of that, she was still drawn to him. More so, as his dark, mesmerising eyes held onto hers yet again, "So, you're really here just to get the lowdown on me?"

"Yes," she lied.

"Why didn't the newspaper just contact my PR company?"

"I honestly don't know," the lies rolled off her tongue, "I was told to come here . . ." How could she tell him she had a shed load of debt and her job was on the line? She wouldn't put it past Neil to withhold a reference if she totally spilled the beans about the DNA sample; she might never work as a journalist again. Ed might even take legal action against them. Against *her*.

"It seems your newspaper has gone to a whole load of unnecessary trouble, if you ask me. I don't get it." He was right, it didn't add up. "What about your manuscript? That's part of the debacle too, I take it?"

"No." She was eager he knew that bit was genuine, "Not at all. That is my story. My writing."

"But you're a journalist."

"So were Dickens and Hemingway."

"Well," he smiled, "the writing was good, I'll give you that."

Ruby couldn't help smiling back. "Thanks."

He gave a heavy sigh. "You're getting cold. Do you want to go back inside?"

She shook her head. "I think I'll call it a night."

"Let's get you back to your room, then. I'll walk with you."

Relief flooded through her. The altercation with Daryl was still on her mind – she didn't want to run into him again on her own.

There was no hand-holding this time walking alongside Ed. Earlier, she'd relished the feeling of his large hand holding hers, even though he'd done it to make a point to Daryl. But it had felt pleasant.

"Have dinner with me tomorrow night," he said, taking her completely by surprise, "just you and I, away from here. What do you say?"

Despite her resolve weakening, she couldn't allow that to happen.

"I can't."

"Why not?"

She swallowed, stalling for an excuse. "I don't see the point. We're both leaving soon and won't see each other again. It's been a great week and you've really helped me with my manuscript, so I'm grateful for that. But it's shortly back to normality for me."

"So wouldn't dinner together round the week off nicely? There's a pub not far from here we could go to, a sort of auf wiedersehen."

"Thanks for asking, but I'd rather not."

"How about if I gave you an interview," he stopped walking, "that's what you want, isn't it?"

"An interview?" she was too busy staring at his perfect mouth to comprehend what he was saying.

"Yeah, an interview. You don't have to play games anymore, I'll give you one. I'm sure your boss is expecting you to return with some sort of story on me, so you can ask me anything you want to know over dinner."

Her tummy tightened. His handsome face was so appealing, and his eyes were willing her to say yes. "I'm really not sure."

He sighed. "Well, I'd love to. I'm sure we would have a good time, and you might get a scoop. The offer's there if you change your mind." He continued walking and Ruby followed.

In her mind she was thinking of a different scoop – scooping her up and throwing her on his bed. She prickled at the thought and pulled his coat tighter around her.

They reached the entrance to Lakeside Plus and he held the door open for her. Ruby brushed past him, the aroma of his musky cologne making her prickle again.

Her chest felt heavy as they walked side by side to their rooms. She was still being deceptive. Neil wasn't interested in a story about Ed's life as a novelist, far from it. He was only interested in exposing him, not that she'd achieved anything to help with that. If Ed knew she'd tried swiping his toothbrush, a glass, and a paper cup, all without success, he'd probably laugh in her face and tell her to stick dinner where the sun doesn't shine.

They paused at the door to his room. She removed his coat from round her shoulders and handed it to him, careful not to touch his hand. "Thank you."

He took it from her and held it against himself. Desire was a rare sensation for Ruby, but it ran through her body as she continued the couple of paces to her room, desperately willing him to drag her back, throw her onto his bed and sod everything else.

"Night," she said, tapping her key card. Her heart felt heavy. What harm would dinner do? – it was only a meal. She could pretend to ask a few questions about his life and the following morning leave early and not have to see him ever again. And who knows, she said quietly to the devil on her shoulder, she might even swipe his napkin.

"Night, Ruby," Ed said, disappearing into his room.

"Wait!"

His head popped back out.

"If the offer still stands, dinner tomorrow would be lovely."

He raised an eyebrow, "Good. I can't wait. I've heard they do a great lamb shank."

25.

In her pretty cream bra and matching thong, Ruby positioned herself in the chair opposite the basic fitted unit with the mirror on the wall. With a steady hand, she applied her smoky brown eye-shadow filling the generous lids she'd been blessed with, while carefully emphasising the corner of the top eyelid with a flick of black eye-liner pen. Lashings of mascara completed the look. A quick skim with bronzer and a light pink lip gloss completed the look.She decided to wear her hair loose, so tipped her head upside down, flung it back again to create lift, and gave it a quick spray to ensure the volume would stay in place. With a quick widening of her eyes to check there were no mascara blobs, she was ready. She didn't normally wear much make-up, but turning her head from side to side in the mirror to check what she looked like, she was happy she hadn't overdone it. She wanted to achieve the image of a confident woman opposed to a slapper.

Sitting opposite him on the small intimate table in the pub, Ruby couldn't help but acknowledge how attracted she was to Ed. He'd removed his smart jacket, and looked good in a blue shirt. It had a small logo on the pocket so it no doubt was designer as all his attire appeared to be. Yet, despite being mega rich, he wasn't one bit flashy. She liked that about him – she liked everything about him if she was truthful.

"I'm glad you agreed to dinner," he said, cutting into his lamb, "it's a nice end to the week."

"Yes, it is. This is a lovely meal," she wiped the corner of her mouth on her napkin – the linen napkin – a reminder she'd been thwarted one final time. The elusive sample just wasn't meant to be. So, where did that leave her?

"Garth said the committee eat here occasionally when they come up to the summer school for a meeting."

"It's easy to see why," she forked up some pasta, "the committee have given us a great week, haven't they?"

"Yes, they certainly have."

"And despite our . . . *bumpy* start, I've learned a lot from you, which I know will help with my novel."

"That's good. What will you do with it when it's finished? Try for a publisher?"

She shrugged. "I'm not sure to be honest."

"Well, you've got my email, so if there's anything I can help with, don't hesitate to get in touch."

"Thank you, I will."

"How do I get the feeling that's not true?"

She smiled at his perception. "You're busy, I wouldn't want to be a bother."

"You wouldn't be a bother." His soft eyes were mesmerising. "Anyway, I know I said I'd give you an interview, and that still stands, however, tonight isn't the best time now. I've had some news about a . . . relative from home, and I have to leave tomorrow."

"Oh, I'm sorry. Nothing too serious, I hope."

"I hope not. But it does mean I'm heading back to the US sooner than I would have been. I've told Garth and he's replaced me in Stage Shenanigans so I can head back to London tomorrow after my last session in the morning. I was wondering how you'd feel about doing the interview over Zoom when I'm home? That way you can have some prepared questions and it won't feel so rushed."

"Erm . . ."

"I know your boss will be pressing you for a story, so reassure him we'll definitely do one. Blame me, and explain I've had to leave and it'll be next week. Tell him also," he paused to take a sip of wine, "I insist on seeing the story before it goes into print. Nothing to do with your ability, don't think that for a minute, I've just learned along the way to check things when I can."

She couldn't help but grin.

"What's so funny?"

"I'd never be allowed to write up an interview with you. One of the senior journalists would get that task. I just erm . . . do the groundwork."

"That doesn't sound very fair."

"No, it isn't, but that's the way it is."

"I could have a word with your boss and say I want you to write it personally."

"No! Sorry, I didn't mean to be sharp. I'd rather you didn't have a word with him. I'll speak to him and see what I can do."

"Okay, if you're sure. But I'd like you to write it, you have a great way with words."

"Thank you."

"Seriously, you do. I think your novel has potential. You must promise me you will finish it."

"Yes, I'll try."

He put his knife and fork down. "What is it, why are you so tense? There's no need to be, it's just a meal, and I'm nothing like Daryl, if that's what you're worried about."

"I'm not. Sorry, I wasn't aware I was tense." It was all the lies; she hated it, and her attraction to him. "I think it's more feeling embarrassed about the whole thing really, and you knowing who I am."

"Don't be. I'm a grown up. You've been sent to do a job, and you will do it. We'll just dictate the terms," he winked. He shouldn't have done that, her resolve was already crumbling.

"If you knew how funny that is," she smirked, "I don't get to dictate any terms to my boss."

"Ah, right, I'm getting the picture. You get to interview those nobody else wants to?"

"Spot on."

"So, didn't anyone else want to interview me and you got the short straw?"

God, more lies. "I think it was more who was in between jobs. And my boss knew I was into creative writing so he thought the summer school would suit me."

"So, he's not all bad, then?"

"Let's just say the jury's out on that." Her face felt warm. If he only knew what a few days she'd had, which had resulted in absolutely zilch. But the last thing she wanted to talk about was *bloody* Neil. It was her turn to drink some wine. A big *bloody* gulp. "And before you say I should change jobs, they aren't that easy to get as I don't have lots of experience. And I really need my job. My boyfriend, or ex-boyfriend I should say, disappeared and left me with some debts." Why was she telling him this?

"I see."

"So, I'm doing as I'm told however distasteful I might find it."

"I'm sorry to hear that. Are we talking a massive amount . . . sorry, I don't mean to pry?"

"It's okay. I will manage it," she rolled her eyes, "I'll just be claiming my state pension by the time it's paid off. The annoying thing is, my parents live in Sydney and I'd love a fresh start and to go over there for a year or so, but I can't leave the country owing everything I do. Well, I say I – he's caused it all, not me. He was devious and I took my eye off the ball. Devious and clever, I never spotted a thing until it was too late."

"It sounds a lot for you to contend with. It must have put you off men?"

She flushed at his words. She thought it had, but she couldn't deny her attraction to him.

"Just a bit," she said with a smile.

He tilted his head, "Only temporary, I hope?"

Her tummy was doing cartwheels. She wanted to shout, *yes, as it's all changed since I met you,* but she stayed silent.

He took another sip of wine. "Ruby," he said and looked her in the eye. "I hardly dare say what I want to say, so I'm just going to go for it. I've learned in life to grab the moment." He leaned forward so he was closer and lowered his voice. "Do you feel an attraction between us?"

His intense eyes locked with hers. She could see the glint of gold fleck as his glistened with desire. Now she understood the expression, *come to bed eyes.*

In her mind he was tugging her dress off over her head, and boy it was getting hot in here.

She almost said yes. Almost.

"Maybe," she shrugged, "but there's nothing I want to do about it."

"Why not?" He grinned. "Don't tell me, I think I know."

"You do?"

He nodded. "It's obvious. Much as you'd love me to ravish you, you don't want me exposing your granny knickers."

Ruby nearly choked on her wine as she burst out laughing.

Ed laughed too, a thunderous guffaw, catching the attention of everyone around them.

"Sorry," he said, "I couldn't resist," then, in almost a whisper, "seriously Ruby, I don't care what knickers you're wearing, I know they'll look great . . . on the floor of my room."

He laughed again and Ruby giggled along with him.

He reached across the table and put his big hand over hers.

"I'm really attracted to you, you're incredibly beautiful and I want you. So much so, that it's taken me all my time keeping my hands of you. I understand if you don't want that, but right now, the only thing I can think about is binning dinner and getting a room upstairs."

Was it so wrong to want to experience sex that was mutually fulfilling for once? It wasn't as if she'd ever have to see him again. Her tummy flipped with excitement. Just one night, that's all. Could she? Her mind raced with images of what might be to come . . . she pictured him naked, putting on a condom before . . .

She gasped.

"What is it?" he asked, squeezing her hand.

Now she was slapping a used condom on Neil's desk. *Here's your bloody DNA.*

Her heart was skipping beats as he looked deep into her eyes.

Not quite the DNA sample she really wanted. Could she do such a thing?

She picked up her wine glass and downed the lot in one go.

26.

They let themselves into Lakeside. The sensor lights lit up the corridor as they made their way along to their rooms in silence and paused at his door. He tapped the key and opened it.

One night, Ruby said to herself, that's all. Nobody would ever know.

The door slammed shut behind them and he swiftly pushed her against it. His muscular body was hard as steel against hers, and with his huge hands holding her forearms, he brought his mouth unhurriedly down on hers. The kiss was gentle at first, and as her lips opened to invite him inside. Their lips moved effortlessly together, hardness meeting softness, sending prickling waves of pleasure from her chest to her tummy. She found herself easily matching the pressure as their tongues demanded more.

Glad of that last glass of wine, she felt in a daze, totally overwhelmed by his masculinity as his arms enveloped her and she wrapped hers around his neck. His mouth relentlessly devoured hers and she matched his ferocity.

He eventually broke contact and rested his forehead on hers. His chest heaved, "Tell me to stop now if you don't want this to go any further."

"How much further do you want to go?" she said, then felt like an idiot for asking such a dumb question.

He chuckled, "I want those granny knickers on the floor."

Maybe it was the wine kicking in, or maybe it was to make up for asking a ridiculous question, Ruby grabbed at the new passion-fuelled confidence surging through her, placed a hand against his chest and pushed him away.

Kicking off her shoes, his eyes were all for her as she, slightly awkwardly, reached up under her dress and, with a few tugs and a bit of a shimmy, managed to free up the tiny cream thong she was wearing and push it down to her feet. She stepped out of it and kicked it aside.

Ed's mouth was agape.

She tried to think of something funny to say, but couldn't, Ed was looking serious, like a bull about to charge.

But no. He stepped up to her, took her face in his hands and kissed her again. Ruby's hands found his shirt buttons, kept on kissing him as he shrugged his shirt to the floor.

Heat flooded from him to her and they never stopped kissing as Ed's hands dropped to his belt. He kicked off his shoes and his trousers and pants soon followed.

Pressed up against her, he was naked, apart from maybe his socks, Ruby presumed, and boy could she feel his nakedness, pressing against her tummy.

"Let me," he said, and Ruby lifted her arms as her dress was lifted over her head and dropped to the floor.

Shivers of expectation ran through her as he unhooked her cream bra and it dropped to their feet.

Bare skin against bare skin, Ruby was both excited and nervous all at once, she wasn't exactly the temptress when it came to sex.

"It's a shame," Ed said, "I reckon you would have looked so hot in granny knickers."

He took a step back, then another, and another.

She was right. His beige socks weren't the best. But the rest of him , , , wow!

"Oh," he said, then quickly danced out of his socks.

Ruby realised then that he was looking at her. She almost went to cover herself, but managed to keep her hands by her sides. Should she say something? Do something?

"I knew you'd be stunning," Ed said, taking hold of his impressive manhood.

Ruby swallowed, felt herself clenching.

He stepped back up to her and pulled her into his arms, his erection impossibly hard.

"I want you," he said kissing her again. "I want you so bad," between kisses.

Her hands went in search.

She couldn't help herself.

Couldn't help taking it in both hands and . . .

Ed groaned into her mouth.

Ruby groaned right back and tried hooking a leg over his waist.

"Shit," he said and pulled away.

Ruby felt bereft. Did she do something wrong?

"No condoms," he said, "I wasn't expecting . . ."

Thank God, Ruby thought, she wouldn't be slapping a condom on Neil's desk after all.

"No need," she said, "I'm . . . I'm on the pill."

For a beat there was only their heavy breaths in the room, then it felt like a dream as Ed took her hand and led her to the bed.

He laid on his back and pulled her on top of him, groping at her breasts as she straddled him.

"Ruby . . ." he said as she sunk down onto him, ". . . fuck me."

***

Ruby red was perfect in every way. A little shy, but pushing at her confidence. Ed liked that, as she ground back and forth. He also liked that she had a sense of humour . . .

She moaned just then, eyes closed as she slid up and down.

Ed moaned in response, moved his hands to her waist, gripped her tight and gave her some pleasure, the resulting whimper from Ruby's puffy lips fuelling his desire.

He rolled her to the side and was soon on top of her, her slender legs opening wide for him.

"God, Ruby," he said, "you're so beautiful."

And he wasn't lying. That luscious red hair, those sultry eyes twinkling with mischief. Those puffy lips he just wanted to devour again and again.

"More," those puffy lips said.

Ed didn't care that the headboard was banging off the wall.

Didn't care when Ruby screeched like a demented banshee when she came.

And he didn't care that he chanted her name as he came, like some pumped-up Kaiser Chief.

"Ruby, Ruby, Ruby, Rubyyyyyyyyyyyyyyy . . ."

But he did care for Ruby. He cared when they'd done it once more, taking her from her beautiful behind, followed by Ruby insisting that she rode him.

He held her tight and pulled the covers over when she fell asleep in his arms after her second shrieking orgasm.

Ed chuckled, reached over and switched off the lamp.

Ruby red was perfect in every way.

27.

Pins and needles in her arm woke Ruby. She was wrapped around Ed with her head tucked into his shoulder. She tried to ease herself away so as not to disturb him, and thought she'd been successful as she gently moved towards the edge of the bed. But he opened his eyes, "Good morning, gorgeous."

"Hey," she said, blushing as his eyes found her bare breasts, despite the crazy sex they'd had.

"Where are you off to?"

"Just need the loo."

"Hurry back," Ed said, patting the bed.

"Of course," she scurried away, picking up her underwear and her dress on the way to the bathroom.

She closed the door behind her and took a moment to clear her head. In the cold light of day, did she really want to jump back into bed with this man for more incredible sex?

The flutter in her tummy screamed YES!

Even, dare she say it, her heart said YES!

But then she saw it, sitting on the shelf like a homing beacon.

Ed's electric toothbrush.

Bloody well done! said Neil in her head, patting her on the back. Job done. Job *saved*.

A night of incredible sex didn't stop Ed being Lilly's father. The newspaper was going to expose him and Lilly's future would be taken care of. It had been her job to facilitate that and why she'd been sent to the writers' school, so she had to take the toothbrush. Then she could well and truly get out of there.

She quickly dressed, splashed some water over her face, then reached out her hand – but stopped herself.

Could she . . . after what they'd shared together?

She stepped out of the bathroom and swiped up her shoes and handbag.

"You okay?" Ed looked fabulously sexy with his bare chest, leaning on his arm with a crumpled white sheet only just covering his bottom half. "You're not leaving me already," he scratched his head.

"I'm afraid so, I need to go to my room . . . female, umm . . . stuff."

"Oh . . . right, yeah," he nodded, "okay then." He reached for his watch, "I'll see you at breakfast?"

"Yes, that'd be great."

"Good, 'cause we need to have a proper talk," his eyes looked so sincere, she was tempted to rip her clothes off and jump back into bed with him.

"Sure," she glanced at the sunlight coming through the curtains, "it's almost dawn anyway. I'll see you in a bit."

He winked, "You bet you will."

She hot-footed it out of the room and headed next door to hers. She locked the door before hitching up her dress and taking the toothbrush from the elastic of her thong. She placed it carefully in the evidence bag and sealed it up. With a bit of luck, Ed would doze for another couple of hours which would give her the time to load up her stuff and get the hell out of there. It had been an incredible night, but it was just sex – a one-night stand. They both knew that. And there wasn't a cat in hell's chance of their paths ever crossing again.

28.

It had been ten days since Ruby had fled from the summer school – ten days in which she'd mourned Ed and deeply regretted what she'd done. She gazed round the busy newspaper office. For everyone else, it was just another day at work. People were sauntering in, clutching coffees, with phones glued to their ears, and early risers were already busy at their desks working on their latest articles, while Ruby, sitting at her desk, felt like a lead weight was pressing down on her and getting heavier by the minute. Ed's toothbrush had been sent for analysis and the results were due this morning.

Ruby looked at Sophie sitting opposite. "Why's Neil keeping us waiting so long?"

"God knows, it's typical of him, though. Millicent has been in there for ages, they must have the result by now."

"It's not right," Ruby said, "you of all people should be told first."

"Yeah," Sophie sighed, "but this is *bloody* Neil, he doesn't think like that. But I already know De'Ath is Lilly's father so the DNA result, whenever we do eventually get it, will only confirm that."

"I suppose so. I'm pleased that you're taking it so well. I felt awful not telling you what I was up to."

"Don't be daft, you've actually done me a favour. I'm just glad you slipped past those housekeepers and got his toothbrush. If you hadn't, we'd still be none the wiser. Hey, look, Neil's coming through, and judging by the look on his face, it's the news we've been waiting for."

Neil sauntered into the main office accompanied by Millicent, who made her way to her desk. "Listen up everyone," Neil smiled smugly. The keyboards fell silent, calls were brought to a close, and the office became quiet.

"I've just received confirmation about the DNA sample," he looked directly at Sophie, "Edward De'Ath is Lilly's father."

A few of the staff actually clapped. Despite all the mutterings, Neil carried on. "So, we are going ahead with the story to expose him and I've asked Millicent to begin a draft. Sophie, we need you to confirm how many times you've tried to contact him through your solicitor. I reckon with a tail wind, we'll pull it together and get it into print by the end of the week."

Ruby felt like she'd been kicked in the stomach. Although there was never any doubt that Ed was Lilly's father, she'd been holding her breath since she left the writers' school. She had to ask the question. She put up her hand.

"Yes, Ruby?"

"Is the test one hundred percent accurate?"

Neil shrugged. "Pretty much so, yes."

The confirmation hit her like a sledgehammer.

Neil carried on. "I do want to make a point. While we all know how we were able to confirm De'Ath as the father, that doesn't need to go outside of this office. We'll keep that little nugget between ourselves. At some stage during any legal proceedings, I'd imagine he'll be asked to give a sample for DNA anyway. But at least now we know we can go ahead with our story to expose him."

"I'm sorry, Neil," Lesley, the receptionist came into the office looking flustered, "he walked straight past me, I couldn't stop him."

Ruby's tummy dropped as if she'd plummeted ten floors in a lift. Standing alongside Lesley was the man she'd craved and thought about every single minute since she'd left him in bed at the writers' school.

"The nerve of the man," Sophie whispered, "and you'd do well to shut your mouth, Ruby."

"What the bloody hell . . ." Neil said. But Ed wasn't looking his way, his eyes were on Ruby's. Her heart raced as she devoured him.

"Hello, Ruby."

Her mouth was dry, she tried to moisten her lips, desperately trying to speak, but nothing came out. What could she say? All she wanted to do was run into his arms and tell him how sorry she was.

The penny must have dropped as Neil broke the silence between them. "I think you'd better come into my office, Mr De'Ath, where it's more private."

180

"I haven't come to see you," Ed barely looked his way, "it's Ruby I'm here to see."

The office stared on. Her heart was ready to burst at seeing him again. She didn't want to be pleased to see him . . . but she was. Despite everything, she cared for him. However, she'd deceived him, he wouldn't want her now. She'd be just a one-night stand, exactly the same as Sophie. So, why then was he here? She swallowed "Why are you here, I don't understand?"

"I came to see you."

Neil interrupted, "I must insist we go into my office, people need to get on with their work." He turned to Lesley, "Could you bring us some coffee please."

"Not for me," Ed said. His eyes scanned the room and settled on Sophie, "You're Sophie, I take it?"

Sophie looked flushed and ready to burst, "Of course I am, as you well know."

"I'm afraid I don't."

"Well, you should do, you're the father of my child. That one night we had . . . we have a little girl."

"That wasn't me," Ed said, "I would have remembered."

"We can prove it," Sophie spat, "we have DNA."

"That's enough, Sophie," Neil interjected. "Mr De'Ath, I'm afraid I'm going to have to ask you to leave. None of this has anything to do with the rest of my staff."

Ed looked scornfully at Neil. "You're barking completely up the wrong tree. And let me be clear, you, nor anyone else associated with this newspaper will be running any stories about me." He turned back to Sophie, "The man you slept with, was probably my brother."

"Your brother?" Sophie scowled, "I . . . I don't understand."

"We're identical twins. I suspect he may have posed as me."

She shook her head, "It can't be. What about the DNA?"

"Identical twins, for the most part, have identical DNA, so it's nearly impossible to establish parenthood. I suspect the covert test done without my knowledge is basic. You would need a more sophisticated one which would look at each twin's complete set of DNA to determine if there are any random differences between them. *If* any differences were found, then they could look at which version the child inherited, and verify paternity from that. But I can assure you categorically, I am not your child's father."

"Why would your brother pose as you?" Sophie scowled.

Ed widened his eyes, "Why would you think?"

"That is a terrible thing to do."

"I quite agree, as would printing any of this in the newspaper. I will ensure my brother takes care of his responsibilities, however, if any articles appear in this paper about my brother, or me for that matter, then that will have to be reviewed." He turned to Neil, "I hope I've made myself clear."

Neil's face and neck were flushed as he nodded. All hopes of a scoop, dashed in an instant.

Sophie ran her hand through her hair. "I can't quite believe this is happening. I don't know what to say."

"I'll make sure my brother does the right thing." He turned to Neil, "Now, if Ruby and I could have the use of your office, I'd appreciate it. We have things to discuss."

"Yes, go ahead," Neil said in a deflated voice.

Ruby's legs felt like jelly as she walked the few paces to Neil's office with Ed trailing alongside. Her heart was thumping so fast she was sure it could be seen through her blouse. He hadn't slept with Sophie after all. How could they have got it so wrong? She wanted the ground to open up and swallow her. She wasn't happy about what she'd done in the first place, but now, she felt disgusted with herself and deserved everything she was going to get.

Ed closed the door behind them and leant against it. Ruby stood a few feet away, facing him. Her heart constricted at how gorgeous he looked in a navy jacket, an open necked shirt and fawn chinos.

"Would you like to sit down?" she asked, a tremor running through her voice.

"No, I'm hoping this won't take long."

She took a deep breath in, poised to take whatever he threw at her. She'd been deceitful and lied so he had every right to go ballistic – it was no more than she deserved.

She cleared her throat. "How did you find out . . . about what's been going on?"

"When you disappeared, along with my toothbrush. It did take me a while, though. I just didn't get the significance of you taking it. I called my PA and asked her to check any communication we'd had recently."

"I am so sorry, truly I am. I'm terribly embarrassed about it all. I'd never have done it if I'd have known."

He shrugged, "What's done is done . . . and if you hadn't have come to the writers' school, you and I would never have met."

"So," she frowned, his reaction was nothing like she had been expecting, "you're not angry with me?"

"Nope. Why would I be, it brought us together?"

"Yeah, but it wasn't for real."

"I thought it was. That's why I'm here, Ruby. I want to know if what happened between us was simply to get the specimen, or if any of it really mattered."

"Of course it mattered . . ." her voice trembled, "it meant everything to me."

"Good." Was that relief she saw in his eyes? "Because it affects what happens between us now."

"In what way . . . can you forgive what I did?"

"Easily." His eyes glinted with mischief, "I think it's quite funny really. I knew all along you were up to something, I just couldn't figure out what."

"But you knew when your toothbrush disappeared?"

"It certainly filled in the gaps and jogged a memory. I remembered a solicitor's letter suggesting I'd fathered a child. I knew of course I hadn't."

"And after all that, you're still . . . interested in me?"

His voice softened, "I've never stopped being *interested* in you since the day you reversed into my car."

"You mean you reversed into me," she grinned.

He laughed as he moved towards her, "Whatever."

"I haven't said anything about . . ." she turned her head towards the window to the main office where she could see staff were watching, "what happened between us. I sort of thought of the old adage, what happens in the summer school stays at the summer school. They think I just sneaked into your room while the housekeepers were cleaning."

"I see. Well, any minute now, they'll know it was a bit more than that."

"Why, what's going to happen now?"

"You don't know?" he smiled playfully. "The way I see it, you've a lot of making up to do to me."

"Oh, okay." Her chest felt like it was about to burst open.

"And . . . you still have a novel to complete, so the way I see it is, I think we need to change the narrative."

"In what way?"

"Maybe something along the lines of, *what goes on at the summer school – moves to New York.*"

"New York!?"

"Yep, New York . . . if you're game, that is?"

She put both hands to her mouth. "Game! For a holiday you mean?"

"Yeah . . . initially. But we will have a lot of work to do getting your manuscript in shape."

"Neil wouldn't let me go for long."

"You leave Neil to me. You can have a sabbatical."

"He'd never agree to that."

"I think you'll find he will, otherwise he'll have a lawsuit as long as his arm."

Ruby giggled, "I suppose there is a lot of work to do with my manuscript. And I guess there could be scope for two books, maybe?"

"Ah, now you're talking," he moved in close, his breath warm on her face. "Or perhaps even a trilogy."

She eagerly welcomed his lips as they found hers, and her arms tightened around him.

In the background, the staff in the office erupted into cheers and applause.

"Sounds like we have their approval," Ed said between kisses. "Shame this office doesn't have blinds."

"Why?" Ruby asked, knowing full well why.

"Because I'd close them, and take you over your boss's desk right now."

She kissed his lips, his jaw, his nose. "You can take me now . . . home to pack."

Ed chuckled. "I like the sound of that. Can't wait to get started on your . . . *manuscript.*"

Acknowledgements.

Firstly I'd like to thank my trusted editor John Hudspith for his invaluable help in shaping this book to the genre. The reason for the change of genre from my usual books and the shortness of it is, I originally wrote it as a competition entry. It didn't win, but I loved the story and wanted to share it. I'm pleased to offer it as a light summer read which I sincerely hope makes reader chuckle as much as it did me.

I'd like to thank Jane Dixon-Smith for the beautiful cover she's designed and Colin Ward for formatting. Thanks go as always to my dear family and friends who are always in my corner cheering me on.

To my readers, thank you so much for your continuous support. Any successes I have are as a result of you buying my books or downloading them on Kindle Unlimited – I really couldn't do any of this without you.

If you have enjoyed this book, I'd be so grateful for a rating or review on Amazon – each review gives the book greater exposure, which is always what I'm striving for.

Lastly, but by no means least, thanks to my dear husband John. To him, I'm the best writer in the world . . . he talks sense that man!

Printed in Dunstable, United Kingdom